THE SECRET

THE GAME SERIES PLAN

BOOK 10

CARA DEE

The Secret Plan
Copyright © 2022 by Cara Dee
All rights reserved

Edited by Silently Correcting Your Grammar, LLC.
Formatted by Eliza Rae Services.

WELCOME TO THE GAMES

The Game Series is a BDSM series where romance meets the reality of kink. Sometimes we fall for someone we don't match with, sometimes vanilla business gets in the way of kinky pleasure, and sometimes we have to compromise and push ourselves to overcome trauma and insecurities. No matter what, one thing is certain. This is not a perfect world—and maybe that's why the happily ever after feels so good.

***The Secret Plan is the tenth book in The Game Series**, and it's the official sequel to Their Boy. But considering so many characters cross over in the series, it's recommended to have read all the books leading up to this one.*

PROLOGUE

Kit Damien

"Little Rudolph! The mischief factory on wheels is here!" Colt hollered from downstairs.

"Okay, thank you, Daddy!" I rushed to screw on the caps on the paint jars before I switched off my lamp and hurried out of my hobby room.

Today was going to be *so* fun.

And for me to even think that was proof of how far I'd come these past six months. I was barely shy at all anymore! I had more friends than I could count on all my fingers, I was a total brat, and I had so many plans. I loved, loved, loved that. Almost as much as I loved my Daddies.

I darted down the stairs, past the second floor, all the way to the first, where Lucas waited with my coat. The living room was super cozy now with Christmas decorations everywhere. Rosa had helped us; she had the right touch for it.

1

Lucas smiled. "You realize this outing raises a fair bit of suspicion, yes?"

I grinned impishly and pushed my arms through the sleeves. "How so? We're just gonna buy Christmas gifts for our amazing toppy Tops."

Colt laughed in the kitchen. "Yeah, I'm sure that's all you're gonna do."

It totally was! Sort of!

"Do you have your wallet down here, love?" Lucas asked, poking his head into the kitchen. "Mine's upstairs."

"Sure." Colt joined us in the rush-hour traffic zone between the kitchen, the living room, and the hallway. "You were gonna eat at Macklin's, right?"

"Yes, Sir." I nodded and zipped up my coat. It was freezing outside, but the snow didn't want to stay on the ground just yet. "I've saved so much of my allowance, I'll have you know."

'Cause I wanted to buy them the best presents in the world. But yeah, okay, so I was still going to dip into my bank account, which I thought was understandable. The allowance thing was mostly symbolic—and to keep track of my ice cream spending.

Colt handed me a fifty, which made me look at him all puzzled. "Treat Gael to lunch too."

Oh! "Sometimes I forget you're a Sadist, Daddy." I pocketed the bill. "You're so sugary sweet, you know? Thank you very much."

He furrowed his brow. "I give you lunch money, and you insult me to my face?"

I laughed and hugged him. "Isn't it better I do it to your face than behind your back?"

That made Lucas crack up.

"Fuckin' brat," Colt chuckle-muttered. "Gimme a kiss."

Gladly. I reached up when he dipped down, and I gave him a big smooch.

Then it was time to hurry. My friends were waiting. I had *friends* now.

Lucas and Colt followed me to the door and peered outside, smirking when they saw the teal-colored brat van Noa, Cam, and a new member named Camden were in charge of. But Camden was sort of a hybrid member...? I was fuzzy on the details, but he and his two Daddies lived primarily in Nashville and New York. They weren't in town now.

"Have fun today, sweetheart." Lucas kissed me on the forehead.

"I will. Love you, Daddies!" As I yanked on my mittens, I ran out to catch my ride.

Tate opened the door and smiled. "Hop in, hon."

I beamed back. "Hi!"

Oh gosh, so much fun. Tate was here, and Cam was driving, Noa sat next to him, then Corey and Shay...

"Where are Gael and Archie?" I knew Macklin wasn't joining us till we had lunch at his restaurant.

"Gael canceled—said he wasn't feeling well," Tate answered.

Oh poop. I had to call him later.

"Archie's on Daddy Duty with Greer," Corey responded. "Sloan spent all day yesterday with Kyla and Emma-Jo outside, and now they're sick. They get sick aaaall the time! Not super sick but enough to get cranky and feverish and sleep a lot. So Greer is cuddled up with the girls, and Archie's fussing over Sloan."

Aw, that sounded all kinds of sweet. And I only thought that because I'd recently gotten to experience that with Colt and Lucas. They'd come down with some stomach bug that'd kept them in bed for two days. And they'd been so pitiful and adorable!

After three hours of shopping, we arrived at Macklin's restaurant in Logan Circle, completely famished.

"Right on time." Macklin smiled and gestured toward the stairs. "I've reserved one of the smaller dining rooms for us."

One of the reasons I loved his restaurant. It used to be condos way back, and now it was a popular establishment with several themed dining rooms. It was like coming to a new restaurant every time, depending on the room you ended up in.

We headed up to the second floor and down a hallway, until we reached what Macklin referred to as the lounge. The tables were a little lower, the chairs a little cushier, the lighting a little dimmer. It was perfect!

Two servers joined us, and the moment I sat down and shifted my shopping bags between my feet, a menu was extended to me.

We all made quick work of ordering, and I got a large Coke and a Cuban sandwich with fries. The fries here were the *best*. Because they were double-fried and had some magical garlicky herb mix sprinkled all over.

With that out of the way, I shrugged out of my coat and tuned in to the conversations flowing rapidly around me. Tate and Shay were noting how tired Macklin looked, which... Huh, I thought he looked great. Handsome as always. He had a cute grin and beautiful eyes in a warm brown shade, and somehow he managed to look both ruggedly sexy and adorable.

"How about we don't discuss me at all?" Macklin rolled up the sleeves of his button-down and slumped down across from me. "What I wanna know is why Ivy isn't coming to the Christmas party."

Seriously! I'd been so bummed out. "Neither are Ella and

Penelope. They're celebrating Christmas on the West Coast with family. And Ivy, August, and Ev are going somewhere too."

Macklin turned pensive. "So it's gonna be only men at your place?"

I nodded.

"Sausage fest!" Corey hollered.

Tate and I laughed.

"We might as well show up naked," Noa said. "Oh my God, I'm picturing it..."

"Nobody would be safe," Tate teased.

Noa didn't argue.

"With Noa and Franklin running around, nobody's safe *ever*." Cam waggled his eyebrows.

"Hell, you should've seen them at Macklin's last event." Tate shook his head and exchanged a grin with Macklin. "And *you*...and Jack."

Macklin's grin turned into a lazy smirk. "I'd be more interested in seeing you and him together."

Welp, I suddenly felt very out of place. "Am I the only one not partaking in orgies?"

Shay chuckled on the other side of Tate. "River, Reese, and I were there too, but trust me, I didn't participate a whole lot. They strapped me to a bench, and everyone was given permission to beat the crap out of me."

That sounded like participation to me.

Macklin winked at me. "There's a standing invitation for you and your Tops, honey."

Heat bled onto my cheeks, and I squirmed in my seat. All amused eyes were on me, and I got it. I understood their amusement and assumptions. Everyone thought I was 100% closed with my Daddies, but truth be told, I had curiosities.

As Noa, Corey, and Cam disappeared into a conversation

about holiday plans, I shifted slightly in my seat to address Tate, Macklin, and Shay.

"So you remember the other week when Colt and Greer kissed..."

"Vividly," Tate answered.

Shay nodded.

"I still can't believe I missed that," Macklin grumbled.

Yeah, his loss. Because Jesus Christ.

It'd been for a photo shoot. We were hanging new erotic art on the walls in the club area at the estate in Mclean, and Lucas and I—and Sloan and Corey—had volunteered Colt and Greer for a bondage shoot. So the two of them had been tied up together, and they'd touched and made out and...holy crap, I'd been so horny.

I cleared my throat and fidgeted with the corner of my napkin that was folded around my utensils. "How would one go about experiencing more of that?"

Thankfully, they didn't laugh at me.

Tate cocked his head, his expression curious. "Are you thinking about playtime or opening your relationship?"

I shook my head quickly. "I can't imagine having an open relationship—I depend entirely too much on Lucas and Colt's security and structure. I love what we have. But..." I hesitated here, partly because the different ways a dynamic could take form were just so confusing. "Okay, so, bluntly, I think it was super-hot when Colt and Greer made out. And Colt told me that he and Lucas had sex with Greer—like, way back. And just months ago, I think I would've been jealous to hear about that, but now... Ugh."

"You're what, twenty-two?" Macklin asked, and I confirmed. "Sweetheart, you're gonna change your mind a million times. I'm not saying you can't be certain about your identity where core relationships are concerned, but it'd be weird if some of the details *didn't* change—and Lucas and Colt are fully aware."

I supposed that brought some comfort.

"We've never discussed it at home," I admitted. "I mean, other than Lucas saying I must tell him if things change and if there's something else I wish to explore."

"This qualifies as that." Tate nudged my shoulder with his, and I chuckled. He was right. I was going to bring it up with Lucas and Colt, of course. "What exactly would you be interested in trying out? Where do you think you would draw new lines in the sand?"

Oh my gosh, I had no idea. I scratched my head. "I'm mostly curious about kissing and touching. I don't know." I did know, however, that I didn't want to have sex with another Dom, nor did I want my Daddies to go too far with another sub, and I managed to express that while blushing my butt off.

Shay scratched his chin and shrugged. "Doesn't sound weird to me. We have a lot of boundaries in my dynamic too. River and Reese aren't interested in playing with others whatsoever, but they're voyeurs who sometimes want to see me with others, but not necessarily for sex. We haven't gone that far yet. I mean, our relationships are fairly new still."

That was certainly true.

"It's good to go slow," Macklin agreed with a nod.

That made me think of something. "You and Tate have known Colt, Lucas, and the Tenleys for years. What were they like before Shay and I entered the picture?"

Macklin raised his brows at Tate and went, "Oh boy."

Tate chuckled. "Well, it's interesting to me because—" he flicked a glance my way, then at Shay "—you two happen to be dating our pickiest Doms. Not to say they don't all have high standards, but Lucas and Colt are more traditional, and River and Reese are incredibly protective of each other."

Macklin was in agreement. "Plus, they've always struggled to feel chemistry with outsiders. Believe it or not, but tons of subs have accused Colt and Lucas of being aloof. Obviously not to their faces but online. And I think...yeah, all subs they've played with—except for Ivy, me, and Cam—have left the community due to unrequited feelings."

I knew the last part. Some had even tried to break my Daddies up. And Lucas had mentioned—because I'd asked—that Macklin was the only current member of House Mclean he and Colt had been sexual with. Because of their friendship, what with Macklin having been there from the start and all, they had established trust and liked each other very much. So it'd been a nice way to scratch an itch. Colt had been able to unleash his Sadist on Macklin; Lucas had been his rope rigger for a short while.

"See, when I picture you with them, I don't get jealous," I said. "I get turned on."

Macklin grinned. "You're so fucking sweet. And you have my number... I sure as hell wouldn't be submissive with you."

I snickered and willed the scorching heat in my cheeks to freaking fade away already.

He was so hot.

The servers picked a good time to appear with our sodas and bread baskets. The latter was another item Macklin had nailed like no other. It was a selection of bits and pieces normally used for other meals, but he had a no-waste policy. So the leftover dough and bread from burgers, sandwiches, pizza, and whatever else landed in the fryer for a quick beat. Then the pieces were dusted with a rub-like spice mix before they ended up in a basket for someone's table.

I sank my teeth into the perfect crunch of a baguette endpiece and nearly moaned at the taste. So greasy, so good.

"Is there a Dom in our social group you haven't been with?" Shay asked Macklin.

"That slut does not discriminate." Tate smirked.

Macklin chuckled and shrugged a little. "What can I say, I'm safe. Men know what they get with me."

I tilted my head. "How do you mean safe?"

He removed the straw from his Diet Coke and took a sip. "I mean that I've proven myself to the other founders over the past decade. You—specifically you, the younger subs—gotta understand that you're unicorns. Because most young subs who join kink communities spend a lot of time spreading their insecurities around. Which we don't always think about since our community is pretty focused on age difference. We have a majority of Doms who are into younger men, and bratty boys who are into older Daddies. But the truth is, when we started Mclean House, we wanted to avoid all that. We see what drama has done to other communities—"

"Hear, hear," Corey chimed in, evidently tuning in to our conversation now. "That's why I left Old Town. Relationship drama and jealousy all over the place."

Macklin nodded once. "So then you have Colt and Lucas, River and Reese, Penelope and Ella—plenty of dynamics who just want to chill. Maybe they're looking for a third, maybe their relationship is open—whatever. They wanted a kinky home away from home where they could find similar people. And they end up with an influx of younger subs who are territorial and uncertain, *which isn't weird*," he stressed. "We've all experienced jealousy and uncertainties. It's practically part of growing up."

"But the founders were already grown-up," I deduced.

Macklin inclined his head. "Colt and Lucas didn't want a sub who was trying to break them up. River and Reese didn't want a bottom who tried to trap them with rules based on inse-curities."

"Oh, bless—Emilio," Tate said.

"River and Reese told me about him," Shay added. "He didn't want to work on his insecurities or something."

"Exactly," Macklin replied. "So his relationship with the Tenleys went south before it'd barely begun."

I saw where Macklin was going with this, and I understood my Daddies' reasoning. The founding members of our commu-nity were so darn helpful and generous with their time, but they had limits. If they were going to act as a newbie's guide into kink, that newbie had to at least be respectful and mindful about boundaries.

"Enter *this* guy." Macklin pointed a thumb at himself, making me smile. "I love those men. They've always been there for me. I want them to be happy. I respect limits. I care."

"You're safe," Tate murmured.

"I'm safe," Macklin echoed. Then he glanced between Shay and me. "However your relationships develop, I think it's more important to think about *who* you play with than what you do during play."

Good point. I could already tell that some men would be safer to explore with than others, and that was solely for how I knew them. For instance, I *knew* Greer was a sweetheart. He was also head over heels in love with his own relationship that he shared with Sloan, Archie, and Corey. I trusted Greer. He was safe.

Plus, Corey was so ridiculously sexy! Like, a scene between us...? If he brought Greer, and I brought my Daddies? Oh my God. I felt like we could go further together just because we knew each other the way we did.

Perhaps I would include Archie and Sloan in that fantasy

someday, but for now, I just didn't know them well enough. That was all. They weren't safe yet.

My first impressions were whispering of all good things in the future, though. Sloan struck me as a mix between Lucas and Reese.

When our food arrived, I couldn't quite let go of the topic, even when the others moved on to discuss the next Game and where we'd host it. I didn't know the theme of it yet, so I tuned out. I kept thinking of "safe" men. Other than Greer—and Corey—who would I imagine playing with? Who could I picture my Daddies with?

I took a big bite of my sandwich and slid my gaze to Noa, Cam, and Corey. Was Noa safe? I wasn't sure. He was so wild! And uninhibited. Maybe Cam was more for me. Plus, I knew him well. He'd been my first friend in the community.

Oof, what about Abel and Madigan? My goodness. My stomach tightened at the thought. Madigan was wonderful and wicked, but... Abel was another matter. He was definitely safe. He'd be fun to kiss and touch.

Macklin and Tate?

Safe. Totally safe. I liked them lots. They were like big brothers, and I'd carried a bit of a crush on Macklin since the first time I saw him at a munch.

Shay... I liked him so much too, but he was like Noa. So, so wild and unpredictable during play.

I frowned to myself, realizing I wasn't picturing many Doms. When I thought about playtime with others, it was primarily with subs. Except for Greer. Why was that? Well, Tate and Macklin too. They were switches but would probably be dominant with me—as Macklin had already said.

I had much to ponder. Much to discuss with my Daddies.

After we'd eaten, it was time to get down and dirty with our Secret Santa plans. The party was mere days away, and we still had a lot to do.

"All right, let's go through the list," Tate said.

I wasn't great at being in charge of these things, so I was grateful for his help. Once I'd unfolded my printout, he read from it.

"Noa, you have Colt," he went on. "How are we on that?"

"We're done," Noa replied happily. "I just have to gift wrap the last when I get home, and Cameron's gonna help me."

I couldn't deny I was a little nervous. Nothing was secret about our Secret Santa game; all subs had decided together who was going to give a gift to whom. *I* had suggested Noa give Colt a gift, because they had a super-fun banter going on, and Colt would never see it coming. He was expecting Noa to brat off since that was what they did.

Tate had helped me organize the drawing of names—or couples. He'd made it look like everything was unintentional. So when a Dom received their note with the name of the sub they were paired with, the paper had a web address at the top, to give the impression we'd used one of those random-dot-org places. In reality, we'd spent hours forming our combos. But yeah, Colt and Noa would have one gift exchange. Shay and Kingsley were one couple. Corey and Reese were another.

And it was possible I was very happy about the fact that Greer and I had ended up together in the exchange.

"Kit? Is your gift for Greer ready?" Tate asked next.

"Almost," I replied, glancing quickly at Corey. "We're missing one piece, which we'll sort out tomorrow."

Corey nodded.

Because that was the genius thing about my plan. Our Doms were expecting to be pranked. They believed we were going to be bratty. But we *weren't*. Corey and Archie were mainly in charge of my gift to Greer; they'd decided what I should give him. Just like they had decided what Gael should give to Sloan, just like I had been in charge of Noa's gift to Colt and Cam's gift to Lucas.

Then we had smaller gifts too. Much smaller gifts—with a twenty-dollar budget. So our Doms would receive a main gift and a small gift. I'd finished my small gift for Greer, 'cause his military background made it easy for me to get him something fantastic.

"And Shay, you're done with Kingsley as of today." Tate made a note next to their names.

"Yes, Sir." Shay leaned back and finished his soda.

"Oh, call me that again." Tate's expression was hidden from me as he turned to Shay, but if it was half as wolfish as the sound of his voice...

Shay chuckled and flipped him off instead.

"By the way, Kit, will someone be Santa at your party?" Noa asked.

"I *think* so...?" I asked rather than stated. "Colt told me to not stick my brat nose in sadistic affairs."

In other words, I could only speculate.

"I'd be very surprised if Santa doesn't show up," Macklin said. "We have one every year."

"I didn't attend last year's party," Cam said. "Who was it then?"

"Reese," Tate said. "Macklin the year before. He, uh... showed up naked."

I burst out a laugh.

"Hey, I had on boots and a Santa hat," Macklin replied defensively.

"Oh, that was a dark year," Cam noted with a shudder.

Macklin groaned and scrubbed his hands over his face, so I was naturally very curious.

Tate had the answer. "Mack's worst Walker relapse."

"Last one too," Macklin was quick to add. "I haven't seen him since then."

So, two years? He hadn't seen his own husband in two years? I knew they'd separated long before then. But they'd yet to actually divorce because Macklin couldn't be in the same room as Walker.

"It was right before Christmas," Tate told the rest of us. "He didn't think we'd notice that he was missing every weekend—and then Ivy and Lucas discovered he'd been going up to Boston every Friday after work for over a month."

"Mind you, this was my first year at Mclean," Cam said. "My first couple of months, even. And I showed up at the Christmas party, only to see a drunk, naked Santa telling everyone that love was for idiots."

"Jesus Christ, can we not go there?" Macklin exclaimed.

"I didn't return for *months*," Cam finished with a smirk.

"So where were you when Walker visited this summer?" Shay asked.

"I went on a last-minute cruise by myself," Macklin responded. "But you know what? All that is over and done with. I've turned over a new leaf. I'll have you know I'm dating someone fucking amazing."

Oh really?

"We've heard that before, babe," Tate chuckled.

Macklin shook his head, insistent. "This guy's different. He's very similar to me, and yet...not. We know each other's hang-ups and don't want more than the other can give."

Well, that was good. Macklin deserved the best.

"So, who is he?" Corey asked.

Macklin cleared his throat and smirked faintly. "We'll go public when we're ready, but it isn't completely new. It's been a few months."

"Are you bringing him to Florida?" I wondered.

I was *so* looking forward to our vacation. Colt had recruited his business partner and former Air Force colleague, Ty, to House Mclean, and Ty was *awesome*. He also had a house in South Florida, and in an effort to make new friends, he'd told Colt and Lucas to "invite some people down there" right after Christmas. Aside from my Daddies and me, the Tenley twins were bringing Shay, and Macklin was invited too. And if I remembered correctly, he'd been offered a plus-one.

"I don't think so," Macklin replied. "I've thought about it, but... I don't know. We'll see. I have a few days to decide." He nodded at me. "When are you guys heading down?"

"On the twenty-eighth," I replied.

"Same as me, then," he said. "I thought Lucas said something about y'all visiting Colt's sister's family."

I nodded. "Yeah, that's right after. She's stationed down there."

Everyone was extra excited because Daddy's sister was pregnant again after years of trying. IVF for the win. Uncle Colt was adorable around little Nicole, and now there would soon be one more to wrap him around their finger.

"Sorry to interrupt, but should we get back on track?" Cam asked. "I have to pick up Lucian's dry cleaning in an hour."

Oh crap—yeah, we'd derailed way too much.

We still had more of our secret plan to discuss!

1.

Colt Carter

With ten minutes to spare, I bought a coffee and made my way toward the exit where I was meeting up with Luke. We couldn't get out of this mall hell a minute too soon.

I'd ticked everyone off my list. I was done. Parents, nieces, my sister and brother-in-law, a few friends, one gift for a Secret Santa brat named Noa, and, most importantly, Luke and Kit.

We had one more present for Kit to prepare, but that would have to wait. We couldn't very well give him a puppy a few days before our vacation.

I took a sip of my coffee and tried to spot Luke in the sea of tired mothers, impatient fathers, and screaming ankle biters. Holiday tunes from several stores mingled together and added to the headache-inducing cacophony, and I seriously thanked my lucky stars that the only little one Luke and I were interested in was Kit. I adored my niece—Luke's niece too—but it felt fucking wonderful to be able to hand her back where she belonged at the end of the day.

In just a few months, I'd have a tiny newborn in my arms. I couldn't wait to welcome a new niece or nephew to the world—

and then I was going home again. To my house, with Luke and Kit, where peace and quiet was an actual choice. If I wanted to play loud music, I could. If I wanted to goof off with my boy, I could do that too. If I wanted to nap on the couch, that's what I did.

Just yesterday, I'd seen Tate post something online. A photo with brochures about surrogacy. We were stoked for them, granted. But I just couldn't imagine...

And the army Greer and his three partners were raising? *Hell.*

No.

I finally saw Luke coming out of a store, and I felt a familiar rush of warmth spread through me. Something had happened between us since we'd brought Kit into our fold, and I fucking lived for it. And I didn't really understand it, because we'd been good. Amazing, even. Luke and I had been spared any major crisis in our relationship. We'd never allowed ourselves to doubt what we had. And still, when Kit stumbled into our lives, it was as if every color enhanced. Every feeling intensified. So yeah, that new love feeling—I was reveling in it.

It didn't hurt that Luke was so goddamn beautiful.

I liked watching him when he wasn't aware. Like right now, when he was focused on checking a receipt. He'd exited a high-end men's fashion store, so I assumed he'd bought his pop another shirt. Same thing every year. One shirt, one bottle of brandy. Not entirely unlike me with my own father, who received a bottle of whiskey and something for his garage every year. Since retiring, my old man could spend hours in the garage tinkering on everything from his truck to furniture. He loved fixing things.

This year, I'd gotten him a new power drill.

I grinned faintly and took another swig of coffee as Luke rummaged through his shopping bags. He was missing some-

thing. Something wasn't adding up. Then I saw the relief and how his stance lost tension when he obviously found what he'd been looking for.

My stomach grew tight at another familiar feeling rushing through me. More and more lately, I hated that we couldn't get hitched. Not as a triad. And of course I wanted to take that step with Kit too, but falling head over heels with that boy didn't erase the fact that I'd spent nearly ten years with Luke. Our history was worth celebrating every damn day.

"Let's get a move on, darlin'," I called.

He glanced up and found me quickly. Then he smiled apologetically and hurried over. "Sorry, I thought I'd lost the Secret Santa gift to Cam."

We couldn't have that.

"You ready to go home, hon? You look a little flushed." He touched my cheek.

"It's hotter than hell in here."

"Well, you're wearing your coat..."

Taking it off would just mean I'd have another thing to carry.

"Let's dump our shit in the truck. Then I'm takin' my man out for an early bird special," I decided. We weren't picking up Kit from work for another couple of hours, and he'd begged and pleaded for McDonald's today. We could just do the drive-thru route on the way home later.

Feeling a little nostalgic, I drove us to the Outback Steakhouse we'd gone to a lot when we lived in Alexandria. They had Bloomin' Onions, and they had comfortable booths where we could sit right next to each other. Nuff said.

"We don't do this nearly enough anymore, baby."

"I know." I kissed his cheek. "We're changin' that."

We'd been so focused on establishing new routines with Kit, not just as a triad but how he and I had our thing and how Luke and Kit had their thing too. We thought that was important. And it was. Kit and I, we'd fallen down a rabbit hole of geekery, from building model craft together to reading the same military-themed books. Luke and Kit's "thing" was more focused on little outings and a pinch of domestic servitude. They liked going to museums and shit like that.

That was when I napped on the couch at home.

Somewhere in the shuffle, Luke and I had forgotten our own dynamic that was just ours. Even Kit had pointed it out.

"We're not tellin' Kit he was right, are we?" I pulled a couple bits of fried onion and dipped them in the sauce. "Remember? He told us we spent too little time together as Daddies."

"Oh Christ." Luke chuckled and spread butter on a piece of bread. "Does everything have to be a competition between you two?"

I finished chewing and reached for my beer. "For you to even ask that question..."

He merely shook his head at me, eyes shining with mirth.

I took a swig of my beer, then ducked down real quick to give him a smooch.

Our food arrived shortly after, but I couldn't really look away from Luke. That sucking-like feeling that tightened my stomach had made a swift return, and I felt I had to say something.

Of course, Luke had to take a photo of our meal first, 'cause heaven forbid we ate something without announcing it on Instagram. But okay, I usually liked his captions.

This time was no exception. I received an alert as soon as he'd posted the photo with his favorite filter.

Christmas shopping done. Now an early bird date with my favorite fighter pilot.

I cleared my throat as he put his phone away. "That pilot of yours is gettin' real tired of not bein' able to call you hubby."

That definitely gave me his attention. The surprise on his face was clear as day. Then something softened in his silvery-gray gaze, and his hand found mine under the table. I knew what he was thinking. I could see it. We'd agreed to never go down that road. Or aisle.

When I'd proposed, I'd proposed eternal engagement because we'd still been holding out hope for including a third partner in our relationship. And we had. We'd found a boy who not only completed our dynamic but who made everything I'd felt for Luke grow tenfold.

"I ain't sayin' anythin's gonna change," I said, feeling a bit uncomfortable. "I'm just—I wish I could, you know. I wish there was a way."

He nodded and squeezed my hand, his thumb brushing over the gold band that had his name on the inside. "I do too." He smiled a little and side-eyed me. "Sometimes when I'm at meetings with clients, I'll refer to you as my husband. Call it an indulgence."

I pressed a kiss to his temple and smiled too. That felt good to hear.

"But, Colt—" He inched away and shifted in his seat to face me better. "Do we need a slip of paper from the government? We've already signed every contract we can to protect our rights and our assets. Screw the technicalities on marriage. We can have a ceremony anyway."

I raised a brow, listening.

Luke leaned in and brushed his lips to mine. "We can get married. And one day, when Kit is ready, we'll do it again."

Still listening. This sounded better and better. "Yeah?"

"Yes. And I propose a family-oriented get-together and then a party with our extra family in Mclean."

Fantastic idea.

"Say screw the government again," I murmured.

He laughed softly. "That wasn't what I said."

Right, but— "Humor me."

He smirked. "How about I'll marry you?"

Fuck. Yeah. That was it. "Deal." I kissed him again, feeling tons lighter. We were what mattered. No government or reverend could tell me whether or not I could call the two loves of my life husband. "Can I convince you to take my name too?"

I grinned as he chuckled and nudged me away.

"I'm only half jokin'," I said.

"Oh, I don't believe the joke part for a second, sweetheart." His eyes shone with amusement again, but I focused on the affection in them.

"I guess we could hyphenate," I bargained.

West-Carter. Carter-West. Didn't sound bad at all.

But Luke shook his head and cut into his steak. "I would love to take your name."

Christ. "You're serious? You'd do that for me?"

"I'd do it for *us*, Colt. Because I want to." He gestured his fork at my plate. "Eat before it gets cold."

Well, shit. He'd just made my fucking day.

I listened to him and cut into my own steak, but my mind was fixed. "You're not screwin' with me, are you?"

"Quiet, dear. I'm compiling a list of venues in my head."

I grinned.

Luke's reaction to what we'd decided today bled into the rest of the day. While Kit was munching on chicken nuggets and fries in front of a Christmas movie in the living room, I was finishing Rosa's list in the kitchen, and I had Luke mirroring my every move.

I fucking loved it.

Right now, he was plastered to my back, pressing kisses to my shoulders and spine.

Our song was playing on the Alexa thing...

After I'd checked the rolls in the oven and dumped a shit-ton of mushrooms into a skillet, I turned around and pulled him in for a tight hug. On a normal day, it wasn't easy to get him to move with me, to dance, even to sway a little, but for once, he let me do it.

"You're Mr. Cuddly today, darlin'... Not that I'm complainin'."

He sighed contentedly and kissed my jaw. "I just love you."

I gathered our clasped hands between us and tilted my head, capturing his mouth in a kiss. In my mind, I started calculating how much work I had left before I could move this upstairs to our bed.

Rosa, the housekeeper Kit had grown up with, was supposed to be enjoying her retirement. But she was one of those women who struggled to let go—something I could empathize with—so Kit had set her up with a new workstation in the kitchen of the studio apartment we had in the basement. But rather than cooking for us, she cooked for her community. She was heavily involved in her church, and she volunteered at the local soup kitchen a lot. Kit being the sweetheart that he was had gotten us all involved, if only a little. In short, we contributed with money so she could keep doing what she loved, while the food went to those who actually needed it.

Rosa got to leave her house a couple days a week, and Luke and I didn't have to feel bad about rendering her previous work position totally useless.

Enter Kit's brilliant idea to host a holiday party. Rather, Luke had been downstairs with Rosa, just chatting, and he'd talked about caterers for said holiday party. Christ almighty, Rosa had about blown a fuse at the mere idea. No, no, *she* did the cooking for Christmas—end of story. Followed by cursing in Spanish.

But my mama didn't raise no slouch. If Rosa was cooking, then so was I. I could handle some simpler items, like sides and bread. Hence my list. The party was the day after tomorrow, and I had seven side dishes to make, all of which—according to Rosa—would taste better after a couple days in the fridge.

"Daddies, I'm finished!" Kit yelled.

Luke lifted his forehead from my shoulder. "Then bring the trash here, please."

I kissed my way along his neck, up to his jaw and lips. "We're goin' to bed early tonight."

He shivered and kissed me back. "Ready when you are, Captain."

Of course he was. My perfect cock-whore. "Fuck, how I love you." I had to suppress a growl and the urge to take him right here and now.

"Oh hi, lovebirds!" Kit entered the kitchen and giggled at his own quip. "You're cute when you dance."

I smiled at him. "You can come take over for me. I gotta check the oven."

He hurriedly got rid of his McDonald's trash before he ran over.

I gave Luke a final peck and let our boy swoop in.

"Let's just hug and sway, okay, Daddy?" Kit suggested.

"I think that's a fine plan, my love," Luke responded.

I grinned to myself and decided the rolls were ready to come out. I'd made an extra batch so we could have a few for breakfast tomorrow. And possibly a couple in a few minutes because, damn, they smelled amazing. They just needed some butter and jam.

"Did you have fun at work today?" Luke asked. "You couldn't stop rambling about that...aircraft carrier or whatever it was, so I figured I'd have to ask later."

Aircraft carrier or "whatever." And that was the man I was marrying. Christ. Our boy had kindly bought two models of the USS *Yorktown* for us, and I was looking forward to building it.

"It was fun, I guess." Kit shrugged as I placed the tray on the island. "It's hectic right before a charity function takes place, so..."

I hoped he didn't overexert himself. Kit had jumped right in, it felt like. Going from doing nothing and hiding from life to... doing everything at once. Now he was the assistant to some event planner at a family friend's charity organization.

It was a part-time gig, though, so it was possible I was just overprotective.

Luke asked all the right questions to make sure the boy wasn't shouldering too many responsibilities, and I listened on one ear as I continued ticking items off Rosa's list. The mushrooms were looking good. Couldn't really fail with a shitload of cream and butter, regardless.

By the time I was moving on to another side dish, Luke and Kit had sat down at the island, and I brought them a couple rolls, butter, and the apricot preserves they preferred. I was a blackberry jam kind of man myself.

"Heavens, baby—these are amazing." Luke approved.

"Holy smokes, Daddy!" Kit too.

Full score for me.

Since I was planning on spending the next fifteen or twenty minutes slicing potatoes for a gratin dish Rosa was making tomorrow, I moved my workstation to the island so I didn't have to have my back to them. 'Cause the way I figured, this was a good time to tell Kit about our wedding plans.

I seized the opportunity when their mouths were full of bread and preserves.

"I wov thiff fong!" Okay, food didn't stop Kit from proclaiming his love for the Christmas song that started playing. *Country* Christmas song, to boot. I couldn't be prouder. "Wing-a-ling-a-wing-ding-ding!"

I stared at him as he danced in his seat, this complete goofball with the most gorgeous, silly grin, and I couldn't fucking believe how whipped I was sometimes. Was there anything I wouldn't do to keep him this happy? I wasn't sure.

Luke knew what I was feeling. I could see it on his face. He felt it too.

The boy owned us.

"You clown—Daddy and I have somethin' to tell you," I chuckled.

"Oh yeah?" He grinned and settled down.

Luke merely flashed me a smile, so I reckoned I'd do the talking.

I cleared my throat and began slicing the potatoes. "So we were talkin' today at dinner, and I may have told him I wished I could call him my husband."

The last traces of humor vanished from Kit's expression, and he tilted his head, visibly confused. "Why can't you? We can marry today, Daddy. That law changed, like, forever ago."

Hoo, his definition of forever needed work.

"Not even a twenty-two-year-old can consider 2015 forever ago," Luke pointed out.

"Thank you—" I started saying, but then Luke had to ruin it.

"You have to remember, Kit," he went on, "that you're dating someone who was born just a few short years after the

Stonewall riots. Not me—I'm not that old—but that corn-fed lone star right there." He nodded at me.

I stopped what I was doing and stared incredulously at the bastard.

Kit all but collapsed in a fit of giggles.

Luke could not look more pleased with himself.

"Hey, *pretty boy*, at least I don't omit my age." I cocked a brow, daring him to deny it. "Somewhere along the line, you started shavin' a year or two off our relationship when someone asks how old you were when we met."

I was very comfortable with my forty-five. Luke, however, liked to *indicate* that he was over thirty-five, to gloss over the fact that he was thirty-eight.

"What?" Kit laughed. "He hasn't lied about his age. Daddy's thirty-seven."

Ha! Case in point.

Luke scowled at me before he averted his gaze and cleared his throat.

"Daddy's thirty-eight," I corrected Kit. "It's such a dumb thing to be vague about too. It ain't like his birthday cake won't say thirty-nine next year."

"Oh, *Daddy*, you're so silly!" Kit laughed some more and hugged Luke's bicep. "This is like when Colt said he was six-foot-five when he's actually six-foot-four."

Well, now. That was entirely different. When I'd said that, I'd been focused on impressing Kit. And Luke had called me out in two seconds.

"But don't distract me!" Kit switched gears. "We were discussing why you can't get married. Which you *can*."

Right, since forever ago.

Deep breath.

Luke and I exchanged a wry little grin and buried the hatchet.

"We know we can, sweetheart," he answered patiently. "But the whole point of us staying engaged was because we dreamed of including *you* in our relationship one day. An engagement is something we can be part of, all three of us. That's why Daddy and I are talking about a symbolic ceremony."

Kit scrunched his nose. "Um, I will die of happiness if I can be engaged with y'all, but isn't it weird to have everything on equal ground? Like, we didn't start our relationship with a clean slate. You know? Cuz you two have been together forever—"

"There's that word again." I smirked and dropped two handfuls of sliced potatoes into the bowl. Only a million potatoes to go.

Kit grinned goofily but continued right away. "I'm *serious*. Our commitment as a triad wouldn't be any less real if you two got married, I think. I won't feel left out if that's what you're worried about."

I frowned.

"I guess, in a way... I don't know how to explain it..." He knitted his brows together and pinched his lips. "Okay, it's like this. When I saw Lucas's Insta post today about your date, I was kind of relieved. I've been *telling* you to do more stuff together as Daddies 'cause, guess what, I need my Daddies happy and united. Just like an actual kid wants their parents happy—and parents have to take time to nurture their relationship too, right? Right. I know I'm right. And even though our dynamic is obviously different—for starters, we're consenting adults—the principle is the same, and I'm your responsibility within our lifestyle. Know what I mean?"

I was sure as fuck no longer frowning, that was for certain. I loved every glimpse I got into his brain, his logic, how he made sense of things.

"I'm with you, little darlin'." I nodded.

"Good boy," he replied. I lifted a brow but let it slide.

"Bottom line, I can't think of any better gesture than marriage to encapsulate the significance of your personal relationship—the one you've shared for eight or nine or two thousand years before you met me."

"Eight," Luke said.

I rolled my eyes. "Nine." For chrissakes, we'd been together nearly a year before I became the last founding member of our community.

He puckered his lips at me in a kiss, then wrapped his arms around our boy. "You're amazing, you know that?"

We could agree on that point.

"You're damn sweet too, Kit, but I don't know." It didn't sit right with me. "Everythin' you said, I agree with. The part where our commitment wouldn't be less real—you're right. It wouldn't. But—"

"Oh my gosh, why do you have to ruin it, Daddy?" Kit grated out.

Both my eyebrows flew up at that.

"I *see* why you decided to go with an engagement instead of marriage," he stated. "You were hoping to include a third partner one day, and you did. But I don't want our triad to be this flat relationship where everything is equal—because that's not our lifestyle anyway. Our commitment to one another covers the equality. I want to spend my whole life with you, so you better get at least one hundred years old. Remember when I asked your mom how old your grandparents became? That's why."

I snorted a laugh. Well, if we could go by their ages to determine how long I lived, we were good.

"But anyway." He got back on track again. "Loving you two is not just about loving you as men. It's about loving and protecting your personal relationship. That's what I've come to realize. Cuz when you think about it, you wouldn't be you without the, um, you know, like, your journey together. That's what I'm saying. We wouldn't have what we have today if you and Daddy hadn't spent those nine years together first. It's the exact same thing with our age difference, when you think about it. I can't be drawn to older men and their experience if I'm trying to wipe that away and be like, okay, the three of us are together now, so let's start over and forget that you already have a lot of history together. That history is the whole point."

I...had nothing. I was damn near stunned. Not necessarily surprised, because I'd quickly come to learn Kit was equal parts young and naïve, and wiser than his years. More than that, what he'd just told us was something he'd started showing us early on. Unlike a couple previous subs Luke and I had failed spectacularly with, Kit wasn't trying to be the center of our universe. He wasn't trying to come between us. That boy could be just as protective of us as we were of him.

"I don't know what we'd do without you anymore." Luke enveloped Kit in a tight hug and let out a breath. "You've come so far too, Kit."

He truly fucking had. The insecurities he'd had in the beginning, the self-doubt and the low self-esteem—he'd worked hard to erase most of them. Not many men as young as he was could say the same.

"Duh! Because you make all the difference," Kit said like it was obvious. "You make me want to fight."

And that was where it was at, wasn't it?

I rounded the island to get in on that hug, and I squeezed them both to me. "We're damn proud of you."

"Are you damn engaged to be married also?"

I rumbled a laugh and peppered his face with kisses. "We'll think about it."

He huffed and pushed my cheeks together.

"Am I cute now?" I asked.

He nodded with a grin. "You look like a brat!"

I chuckled and backed away. "One brat in this house is enough."

"So when are you moving out?" Luke asked.

Hateful. "Real nice—"

"Oh! One thing, one thing, one thing," Kit said urgently. All of a sudden, he was fidgety and nowhere near as confident as before. "Can you maybe not be gone on your honeymoon for too long? 'Cause I will miss you."

Jesus Christ. I was just about to open my mouth when Luke beat me to it.

"First of all, we haven't decided anything," he told Kit. "Second of all, you're out of your mind if you think we'd leave on a honeymoon without you."

"Damn right." I nodded firmly. "We're a family, Kit. We travel together. It's one thing if we spend the night separately whenever one of us is working late—like you and I have stayed at the cabin a couple times when Luke couldn't get off from work."

"Or when you and I stayed there when Colt was at Langley," Luke added. "But there is no way I'm going on a vacation without either of you."

The relief in Kit's eyes allowed me to relax too, and he leaned against Luke. "Okay. I like that."

Good. That was settled.

2.

"**S**o itchy!" Kit tried to squirm away from me and tuck the duvet in between us, but I was having none of it. He'd played an active part in having my chest fucking shaved for a bondage photo shoot the other week, so I reckoned he deserved to suffer the aftermath of feeling my hair grow back.

"What'd'ya expect, huh?" I growled playfully against his smooth stomach before I rolled on top of him and rubbed my chest over his.

"Oh noooo!" he laughed through a groan. "Daddy, save me! Lucas! Ugh!"

How convenient I heard the toilet flushing on the other side of the wall just then.

"I will bite your butt!" Kit threatened.

"How are you gonna reach it?" I nipped at his jaw. I had no issue reaching his butt, on the other hand. I just slipped a hand under him and groped all I wanted. "You probably don't wanna get yourself into unnecessary trouble, considerin' that's all you'll be doin' tomorrow."

Greer was bringing his brood over right after they'd dropped a few kids off at day care and school, and knowing Kit and Corey... There would be trouble.

"Will *not!*" he insisted. "We're just gonna decorate Christmas cookies."

I smirked and kissed him. "Right, and your Secret Santa game will just be about exchanging gifts too."

He grinned like the little devil he was. "Well, yeah. What else would it be about?"

I narrowed my eyes. We didn't know what the boys were planning, but we were prepared for anything. We had a plan B.

Hearing Luke leaving the bathroom, I gave Kit another kiss before I returned to my side of the bed. I had more questions about the Secret Santa exchange, but I could be patient sometimes. It was part of the fun to see if they could throw us off our game.

When I'd spoken to Greer yesterday, we'd theorized a little, and we'd decided tomorrow would be a good day to do some digging. Archie had apparently spent two days baking up a storm, so they were bringing a bunch of it here so the brats could decorate cookies together. Archie wasn't staying long; he was taking their youngest out for Christmas shopping with his sister, but Corey and Kit would be in the kitchen, supervised by Luke and Sloan. Meanwhile, Greer and I were gonna listen in and tend to final preparations for the party.

With only Sloan and Luke nearby, Corey and Kit might lower their guards a bit.

"Ivy's morning sickness has worn off," Luke mentioned as he joined us. "I'm going to miss her this holiday."

Yeah, me too. But a fairly large crowd in our community left town over Christmas. Many of us had family in other parts of the country. Hell, Luke and I were usually with his folks or mine.

"Just keep your focus on me, and you won't miss anyone, darlin'." I stretched out comfortably and slipped a hand under my head.

Kit snorted at me. "Can you imagine if I responded like that, Daddy?"

Luke shook his head, amused. "One cocky pilot is enough, don't you think?"

"Yeah," Kit laughed. Then he turned his head to me. "But we love you anyway."

"Of course you do. I'm irresistible." I winked.

"Lord." Luke returned his reading glasses to the case on the nightstand, proceeding with his little nighttime routine. Another one I liked to watch when he wasn't paying attention. He was such a creature of habit—from the cereal he ate for breakfast to how, fifty percent of the time, he forgot those glasses in the bathroom and had to go back for them.

He'd recently showered too, and for some reason, he always put on his slippers—when it was cold out—his flannel bottoms, and a white tee, even though he'd take it all off a couple minutes later when he snuck under the covers.

"Is it story time now?" Kit yawned and pulled the duvet up to his chin. "I want to hear about the reindeer."

"Hmm, okay. Bedtime story with Santa's reindeer." Luke turned pensive and got comfortable next to our boy.

This had become the highlight of December for me. Every night, Luke had improvised a short, Christmas-themed bedtime story for Kit, serving as another reminder of how much our lives had changed since last winter.

I turned off the light on my side and yawned too. Completely blissed out. Kit's hand found mine under the duvet, and I gave his a little squeeze.

"I suppose I can tell you about the year Santa almost fell off his sleigh," Luke offered.

"Gosh, yes." Kit was hooked already.

I grinned sleepily. Before Kit, I'd had no idea Luke was such a good storyteller.

This needed to be a new tradition for December, where I became his very willing audience.

"I remember it like it was yesterday," Luke went on. "I saw it with my own two eyes. I was in third or fourth grade, and I would sneak out to my treehouse in the middle of the night to see Santa land on the roof with all his presents."

I let out a long breath of utter contentment and felt his imagery sweep me away.

"That had to be super cold," Kit said.

"I brought my coat and hot chocolate, obviously," Luke added.

"Oh, good. That's so yummy. And blankets?"

"Three of them," Luke confirmed. "And never in a million years had I thought I'd be ready to use those blankets to save Santa's life. But that night, as my nose got colder and my toes started numbing, I heard the faint sound of bells in the air, followed by a distant 'Ho, ho, ho! Easy now, Prancer. Careful, careful!' I immediately knew it was Santa and that he was in trouble."

I yawned again and glanced over at Luke.

"The entire sleigh was shaking and skidding across the sky," he said. "Then Vixen came to an abrupt stop right as they reached my street, and I watched the sleigh almost flip forward —and Santa was nearly catapulted from it. So I grabbed my blankets and rushed down the tree, then darted out on the street."

Maybe Vixen was sick of Prancer's bullshit?

"Then what happened, Daddy?" Kit pressed urgently.

"Rudolph came to the rescue." Luke smiled. "He did some sort of maneuver that prevented Santa from falling."

Some sort of maneuver.

My mouth twitched.

To no one's surprise—well, at least not mine—the word

maneuver got Kit going. "What kind of maneuver?" He sat straight up and cocked his head. "Oh! What happens when Santa has to deliver presents at military bases? Because we *know* Daddy would've shot Santa down. Some alarm would've sounded, and Daddy and his wingmen would've run out on the taxiway and lifted in two seconds!"

I rumbled a chuckle as he got more and more animated.

Next, he deepened in his voice and imitated static over the coms. "Prrrcht, we got a bogey. I repeat, we have visual on a bogey. Tshhht—or, wait! Would that be a bandit once you have a visual?" He didn't let me respond before he continued excitedly. "What was that, Sir? We're clear to take 'em out? Sir, yes, sir! Target locked, target locked. Sayonara, you jolly old cookie thief—you've climbed down your last chimney! Boom!" He made an explosion sound, but that was clearly not enough. He started gesturing too. "And then a few A-10s join Daddy, and they go brrrrrt, brrrrrrt! Die, Santa, die! And the reindeer you rode in on!"

"Jesus." I coughed through a laugh, unable to help myself. He was too fucking funny.

Luke, on the other hand, stared blankly at our boy before he turned to me and just said, "I have concerns."

That only made me crack up more.

"What!" Kit demanded, out of breath. "They didn't have a permit to fly there."

I laughed. "So I reckon this is the story of when Santa fucked around and found out."

"Yeah!" Kit grinned widely.

Luke gave us the "You need Jesus" look and shook his head.

"This was fun. Can't wait to see what tomorrow's bedtime story is about," I said.

"Maybe something sweeter?" Kit suggested. "Daddy sure picked a gruesome story tonight."

I had to agree.

At a little past eight the next morning, commotion filled the entryway when Greer arrived with his family.

"Oh my gosh, he made *so* many cookies," Corey gushed. "Didn't you, Archie?"

"You can put your mittens here, little one," Lucas said.

"I can't wait to see them!" Kit replied. Our boy was excited. "Lucas and Rosa prepared a bunch of things in the kitchen we can decorate with."

"Daddy, I wanna change into my jammies right away." That was Corey again.

"They're in your backpack, baby." And that was Sloan.

I tightened the drawstrings on my sweats on my way down the stairs, already certain I'd made the right call to put on long johns underneath. Snow was falling outside, and the gust of frigid air that traveled from the hallway showed no mercy.

The living room radiated warmth and coziness, from the fireplace to the Christmas tree, all the decorations and piles of gifts, and here I was, heading out for a run in a goddamn blizzard. But when Greer had suggested it, I hadn't even hesitated. It'd do me good to get some cardio in before Christmas food filled my belly.

Most of the time, Ty and I worked out at a gym near our headquarters, lifting weights and whatnot. I couldn't remember the last time I went out for a run. Had to be months ago anyway.

Speaking of Ty—I made a mental note to call him later. He was heading down to Florida tomorrow, and I wanted him to bring the applications we'd received for three positions we were looking to fill. We couldn't very well run a private security business without employing private security. We'd gotten a good, solid start with alarm systems and technology; now we wanted to take MadCo Sec to the next level.

"Catch me, Papa Bear!"

I joined everyone else in the entryway just as Corey jumped into Greer's arms and smooched him on the cheek with a silly grin on his face.

"Are you gonna run with Mister Colt now?" Corey asked.

"Mornin', y'all," I said.

They turned my way with a handful of greetings, and Greer responded, "Aye, I gotta see if Colt's still got it."

I smirked and reached for one of my beanies.

"My Daddy's the whole package with a big package," Kit said matter-of-factly.

I laughed. That was my boy.

"Oh yeah?" Corey gave me a once-over and waggled his eyebrows.

Such a little flirt.

"Well, this could take forever," Luke drawled. "May I suggest breakfast in the kitchen while the coffee's hot?"

I chuckled and stole a quick kiss before I squeezed by.

It seemed Greer had opted for similar clothing; I spotted a skintight undershirt when he replaced his coat with a hoodie, and I doubted he was freeballin' it under his sweats.

The boys chatted excitedly about the day as they left the hallway, and Luke informed me Reese would stop by with the Tenley's annual Band-Aid gift soon. I nodded in acknowledgment and finished tying my sneakers, wondering how far "water-resistant" was gonna get me in this weather.

Soon enough, Greer and I were out the door, and we decided to head down toward the waterfront. The sidewalks were likelier to be better tended to there than here, where the strips for pedestrians were so narrow you could barely walk side by side.

Perhaps "blizzard" had been a stretch, but it was cold as fuck and snowing quite a bit.

"You stayin' in Winchester over the holidays?" I asked.

"For Christmas." He nodded with a dip of his chin. "We'll head up to my folks' over New Year's."

Nice. I reckoned it'd be the official introduction of his three new partners to his big New York family. I'd learned Sloan didn't have much family left. Archie's parents lived in the UK. Corey was a local, but if I remembered correctly, his dad lived in Costa Rica or something.

We crossed the busy M Street in a fast jog, which reminded me I had to pick up Luke's order at Sprinkles when they opened. Both he and Kit had decided they were in a red velvet mood today.

It'd be a cold day in hell before I ate red velvet cake outside Texas and the South.

To be honest, it'd be a cold day in hell before I bought a cupcake for five fucking bucks.

"Remind me to swing by the cupcake joint on the way back," I said. "Luke and Kit love to spend a fortune there."

"Christ—don't get me started," Greer huffed. "We stopped at a donut place on our way to the city. Corey doesn't even look at price tags. I love the kid with all my heart, but if you shell out four dollars for some marked-up Christmas donut without batting an eyelash, you're a city boy through and through. And that's comin' from me."

Well, Greer had left his big-city-isms behind a long time ago. He and I had a lot in common—and neither of us struggled financially—but that didn't mean we couldn't see the outrage in city prices.

We had another thing in common too. Our Littles were well-off. Kit was the mother of all trust fund babies, and Corey had made an impressive living out of illustrating some comic strip online for neurodiverse people.

"Do you feel like you gotta hold back the discipline sometimes?" Greer asked. "For the first time since Corey joined us, he's been regressing a bit—mostly with Sloan, but it doesn't really stay there."

I knew what he was talking about. I sucked in a cold breath and kept my eyes on the pavement. Sand and snow crunched under my feet, and the sidewalks in Georgetown were famously unlevel.

"He loves to shop when he's in his little space," Greer admitted, and I had to laugh. "Yesterday, his gifts for the kids started to arrive. I'm tellin' you, Colt—I wanted to tan his goddamn hide as much as I wanted to hug him half to death. He bought Jamie a fucking four-wheeler for kids. He set a thousand-dollar budget for each of them."

"Oof." I winced and chuckled.

"Thing is, he doesn't see the money," he went on. "He's pretty much done building a connection with them—they all adore him because he's funny and sweet. This isn't him sucking up to Sloan's children or anything like that. He just sees things he thinks the kids will love, and he goes with it."

Kit was the same way.

"Yeah, you can't really reprimand that behavior," I said, my breaths coming out faster. "When Kit goes nuts with his spending, Luke and I sit him down once the excitement has blown over. We let him have his fun, and then we try to explain our side. No, he doesn't need to buy ten boxes of model crafts in one go when nine of them will end up on the shelves. No, we don't need to order everything on the menu because a brat can't decide what he wants for dinner. No, we sure as shit don't need to buy a sixty-five-inch flat-screen for every guest room." I nodded in acknowledgment as

Greer veered left for a narrow backstreet. "He's gotten a lot better at talking to us when one of those impulses strikes—like the damn flat-screens—but we still come home to surprises here and there."

I understood Greer's struggle because Corey and Kit were genuine sweethearts. They loved to make others happy. Kit's shopping habits were more often than not related to making another person smile. Or with the TVs—he wanted to be a good host and have his loved ones return. And the point Luke and I tried to make was, one, a flat-screen wasn't the way to do that.

On our detour along smaller streets toward the waterfront, I explained how Luke and I simply tried to maintain a balance between what was reasonable and sustainable, what might promote unhealthy behavior, and what money could and couldn't solve.

Kit had lost his parents; he'd lived a sheltered life, and he'd had very few friends up until this summer. Corey suffered from some abandonment issues from a Dom who'd fooled us all. Which still fucking infuriated me. We hadn't seen the abuse for two years. So the boy sometimes felt like he was in the way.

"I suspect their habits come from a similar place," I said. "At least sometimes. Make everything perfect so that no one leaves."

Greer nodded once. "Not a day goes by when I don't wanna bash Marcus's skull in."

That would be the ex who'd used and abused Corey.

"I feel ya, buddy." I dragged a hand over my face, wiping away the snowflakes as they melted into ice-cold water. "But—so, when Corey drops a fortune on somethin' for someone else, just...you know, remind him he doesn't have to. At least, that's what we do with Kit. And you know what? Nothin' wrong with a little bit of punishment for those acts. By now, Kit knows he's not allowed to buy affection. He'll slide down some slope of insecurities—it's rare now, thankfully—and he'll think someone will like him more if he brings somethin' extra. Trust me, I have no issues givin' him the belt for those occasions. Just—I'll let the talk sink in first, and I'll tell him we don't want to encourage that line of thinkin'."

"That's the route Sloan took yesterday." Greer was becoming out of breath too, thank fuck. "Not with the belt, but how he explained the reasoning behind the spending and how we don't want him to use his money for everything. Jamie lights right up—all Corey has to do is tell some funny story about frogs. Emma-Jo is weirdly attached to both him and Archie. I mean, it's happened so fast, is all. But either way...yeah, the shopping has to go down. *I* was the one who wanted to give him the belt, but he was in his little space, so I let Sloan handle it."

Probably wise. It was a tricky balance, especially when the boys regressed. "Sometimes it's better to save the punishment for after. With Kit, it can go both ways—as long as I don't throw him off. Like I said, we discuss it."

"Makes sense. That Daddy business is fuckin' new to me."

I chuckled breathlessly, every gust of air misting in front of me. "Don't sell yourself short. You've been a Daddy to half the community for eight years."

He snorted.

"I mean it. You realize the brats laugh at you when you claim that fetish ain't for you?"

"Let them fuckin' laugh." He got a little huffy. "Goddamn brats. What do they know?"

I smirked and sped up a little. We were almost at the river. "Greer, my boy wouldn't have a li'l crush on you if you weren't a Daddy type."

"Aw, shit—really? He's too sweet, that one." He grinned and sniffled. "Don't let Corey know. He's been complaining about youse being a closed triad since the bondage shoot."

Funny he should mention the photo shoot. We'd clearly opened a can of worms. And maybe I was ultimately the guilty one since I'd told Kit about the time—way, way back—when Luke and I had a threesome with Greer.

"I reckon *closed* will be a relative term soon enough," I admitted. We slowed down before we reached a stoplight. Traffic was nuts down here. I blew out a heavy breath and eyed the lights, waiting for it to turn green.

"You kiddin'?" Greer was surprised.

I couldn't blame him. Luke and I had always been restrictive in how we played.

I wiped sweat off my forehead and rolled my shoulders. "Kit's twenty-two years old, man. He'll wanna explore a little bit. We think he's gearin' up to talk to us about it."

Boy thought he was being subtle about it too.

"You okay with that?"

I flicked him a sideways glance before I returned my gaze to the light. And at the tightening of discomfort in my stomach, I had to chuckle at myself. "I will be. He ain't the type to finally discover he wants several relationships."

"But that's what's runnin' through your head," Greer deduced.

Well, yeah. "I know I'm worryin' for nothin'."

"You really fucking are, buddy. Let's go." The light turned, and he took the lead across the street.

Having no interest in the tourist attractions along the waterside, mainly the ice rink, we headed straight for the narrow waterfront park that extended along the river.

We weren't the only ones running here, but I'd expected more.

The trees were actually covered in snow. It wasn't melting as soon as it hit the ground anymore.

"As someone who just had his pipe dreams come true," Greer said, "lemme remind you of back in the day when you and Lucas talked the future. How you wanted your own Little,

44

then friends with similar tastes y'all could meet up with for dirty playdates."

Reality looked a lot different from fantasies.

"It never stays at that, though," I replied. "You know how it is. You have a few drinks with your friends and you conjure all these dream scenarios, and...that's it."

Way back in the day, as Greer had mentioned, Luke and I had been naïve as hell. Sure, it was hot in theory—share a playtime dynamic between two established relationships. But...I just couldn't picture it today. I wasn't that man anymore. I had no interest in sticking my shit into someone other than Luke and Kit, which I told Greer.

"Who says you have to?" he retorted. "From what Corey's told me, Kit's more interested in seeing Tops together. He kept talkin' about you and me last time they met up."

"If you're volunteerin' your ass, I might reconsider."

He barked out a gruff laugh that made me grin.

"What else did Corey tell you?" 'Cause that was a more important question. So far, Kit had only danced around the subject with Luke and me—and a single question wasn't enough to raise suspicion. It was when we gathered them all that we saw something was on his mind. Like, what kind of Daddy did Luke and I believe Sloan was? Was any part of Macklin on the Little spectrum? What kinds of subs did Tate like to top when his inner switch wanted to be dominant? Were Cam and Lucian monogamous? Was Macklin good at being dominant?

"Not a whole lot," Greer replied. "Sloan isn't interested in being with anyone outside our family right now, but he gives Corey his full support to pursue playtime with others as long as I'm there—so it's me the boy comes to. Whenever he's got a fantasy about another member in the community, he brings all his questions to me. And most recently, it's been Kit."

I reckoned that made sense. Other than Corey having a higher threshold for pain, they were similar as Littles.

"You know, if it stayed there, I wouldn't mind one fuckin' bit." I swallowed against the dryness in my throat and sidestepped a pile of frozen dog shit in the middle of the path. Real nice. "Hell, I can easily picture havin' you and Corey over for dinner and then we let them play together."

That was part of why I knew I was worrying for nothing, because Kit had only inquired about people I trusted completely. Like Tate and Macklin. If Kit wanted to explore something casual with them, I'd be fine with that. I'd reap some rewards too, hopefully by being able to whip the fuck out of Mack's ass or just watch Tate seduce Kit.

Greer furrowed his brow. "So where do you draw the line personally?"

That one was easy. "I don't wanna play with other Littles. That ain't a hat I can don for just anybody. But that's *me*. I wouldn't mind seein' Luke with, say, Corey. For one of those playdate scenarios. Call me weird, but..." I trailed off and frowned to myself.

It was getting increasingly difficult to keep up a conversation when my breathing turned more and more labored. And we hadn't completed half our run yet, if we were planning on circling the park a couple times and then running back home.

At least I wasn't freezing. Blood was pumping; sweat was running.

"You're not weird, Colt. Well, not for that reason anyway."

I chuckled.

"It's interesting you have other limits for Lucas," he pointed out.

Was it, though?

"He's a Daddy through and through," I replied. "Just like my personality screams Sadist. I can be a Sadist for anyone offerin' up their ass. Bein' a Daddy—and bein' intimate with a Little—is private to me. That's why—" I had to pause to get air into my lungs. Goddamn. It was way too soon to start panting. "I mean, you and me at the photo shoot. Kit and Luke weren't the only ones who enjoyed us makin' out. But I wasn't your Daddy. You weren't in a vulnerable state of mind. I didn't have to worry about your boundaries."

"That's true," he conceded. "I get that. I can relate to an extent."

Of course. We all had sides to ourselves we only shared with a select few.

Spotting one of those gazebo-type pop-up cafés up ahead, I suggested we go there to buy water. I was fucking parched.

"All right, so where are your limits for Kit?" he pressed.

That was the question, wasn't it?

"Strictly speakin' of my personal comfort?"

He nodded.

"Well..." I blew out a heavy breath, jogging past a woman with a stroller. "I guess I kinda apply the same rules to him that I do to myself. If he wanted to play with other Littles, that's fine. Just like I imagine him thinkin' it's fine that Luke and I play with other Tops. But if he wanted to get intimate with a Dom outside our triad...? Damn. I don't know. It depends who."

"Me."

I shot him a bitchy look. He was pushing hard now, goddammit.

He merely smiled.

Then he chuckled. "Come on, Colt. You can't honestly say you'd be worried. I'm not tryin'a be a dick—"

"No, that comes naturally."

"Ha! Fine. I'll knock it off."

Thanks.

Fucker. We ran the last stretch in silence, and I patted my

pockets, only to remember I'd stuck a ten-dollar bill down my left sock. They better accept cash at this place.

Six or seven tables were scattered outside the café, all filled with families enjoying a hot beverage in the freezing weather.

"You want something other than water?" Greer asked.

I came to a stop a few feet away from the short line and shook my head.

"You stay here. I'll get it," he said.

I was too out of breath to speak, and I couldn't shake the unease from our conversation. Worrying for nothing, worrying for nothing. I kept repeating those words to myself, all while wondering why I was being such a stick-in-the-mud. Because even though I'd always been somewhat traditional with my relationship thinkin', I felt almost rigid now.

But it was Kit. He made the difference. I was literally more than twice his age, and I guessed it brought a bit of worry to think he might change his mind. Which—fucking of course he would. Me at twenty-two was nothing like me at forty-five.

I scrubbed my hands over my face and turned away from the people.

There came a time in every relationship with a significant age difference when the partners had to consider the future more seriously. When someone acknowledged that, when Kit was forty-five, I'd be nearing seventy. And that was just an epic clusterfuck of anxiety that formed a fist around my gut. Christ almighty.

Then I heard Luke's voice in my head. It was over twenty years till then.

"Fuck," I exhaled.

I looked up between the trees. Traffic on one side, the river on the other. Yet, we had this sliver of nature in the middle of the city, where children played with a dog and mothers hollered to the kids that their cocoa was getting cold.

In the end, as long as we made it that far... I had to think of the grand scheme of things. If I held Kit back, I might not get to whoop his ass at forty-five.

Fuck, I bet he'd be just as cute then. I could practically picture him. And us. With graying hair and laugh lines, his smile would still be boyish. His eyes would still show mischief.

I cleared my throat and swallowed hard.

I wasn't gonna worry. It was fucking stupid. I'd done the same with Luke in the beginning, what with me being away on deployments and all. Those two—they were the only ones who had that power over me.

What was even stupider was when I shared some of the fears we'd worked so hard to eliminate with Kit. How many times had I told him to relax and have a little faith? We were gonna make it. We were fantastic together. We loved each other so goddamn hard. And here I was, doubting, worrying...

When, in reality, I wasn't sure I had anything to worry about at all. Not more than what was okay. The future wasn't written in stone, and it wasn't supposed to be. I didn't want it to be either.

It was true what Luke and I had told Kit. We'd struggled to connect with Littles in the past. We'd had a hard time finding someone we had good chemistry with. But that didn't mean Luke and I hadn't been able to let go and have some fun with buddies from time to time, even though it'd been years. Greer wasn't the only Top whose cock Luke had deep-throated while I'd fucked him from behind. Who's to say we couldn't do that now? Particularly if we had a boy curious about exploring group play.

Finally, I got my breathing under control. Heart rate returned to normal.

I felt better by the time Greer appeared with two overpriced bottles of water.

"Don't tell me what it cost," I said. "Just take money from my wallet when we get back."

He chuckled and took a swig of his.

I followed suit, not stopping until I'd chugged half the bottle.

"I'm sorry if I came on too strong earlier, buddy."

I shook my head and wiped my mouth. "You didn't. I needed to get my head screwed on right, is all. You have almost ten years with a person, and suddenly you're a pro at a new relationship with another."

Unfortunately, life didn't work that way. I was still a beginner with Kit.

"Easy to get blinded, I bet," he said. "For what it's worth, I've never gotten the impression that Kit wants to open your relationship."

Neither had I. Which was why it was extra vital I didn't hold him back or suffocate him. Especially with rules I didn't fucking want to apply anyway. Group play could be fucking intoxicating in the best way—provided we trusted the people we played with.

After finishing my water, I threw the bottle in the nearest recycling bin. "So...as a Dom in those situations—when Corey or Archie come to you wantin'a play with someone else, how do you go about it?"

Greer smirked a little. "I check my own interest. If it's there, I approach the Top of the little one Corey wants to get down and dirty with, and if Colt agrees, that's what we'll do."

I grinned. "You know how to butter me up, sugar."

"It's a skill." He threw away his own bottle, then nodded up the trail. "Shall we?"

Yeah. I hadn't keeled over so far, so I liked my chances.

"I'll talk to Luke when we get back," I said. "I'm sure he's interested. My city boy was always more liberal than me."

"Liberal," Greer chuckled.

We picked up the pace and hit another path in the park, one a little closer to the water.

"Don't get me wrong, Colt. I understand the trepidation. We've seen too many relationships go down because of various degrees of openness."

True, but that was more often than not due to shitty communication and insecurities. Just look at Tate and Kingsley. They'd almost lost the best damn thing they'd ever had—each other. But they'd made it. I'd never seen them so love-sick before as they were now.

Nathan and Ash hadn't made it, and that sucked. I'd been fairly close to Ash, but he'd left the community when he and Nathan divorced last year. It'd hit kinda close to home, too, since they were like Luke and me. Two Tops who hadn't been able to let go of each other. Nathan, a rope rigger. Not unlike Luke, though Nathan was definitely in a league of his own. Bondage was his life. And Ash, a Sadist and primal player.

They had kids together, to boot.

"Call me Team Ash, but I don't see Nathan's new boy makin' it with us in the long run," I said.

Greer turned to me and raised a brow, but then he got it. He understood how I'd gone from point A to point B. "I dug Ash too. Nathan was never really..."

Yeah, he hadn't been part of our circle. He stuck to the bondage crowd—but maybe that was changing. I didn't know. We'd seen him more often since the fire, though. He'd really come through on the volunteering, that was for damn sure. He'd offered his services as a psychologist to anyone who needed to talk about the fire. I knew Corey had weekly sessions with him.

"He's hot as fuck, though," Greer said. "I kinda wanna see him tie up Archie in one of those suspension-type positions. I'd just sit there and watch."

I'd grow restless in a minute. I definitely saw the beauty in the finished work; bondage photography was a personal favorite, and we had a couple coffee table books with that at home. But just sitting there watching? Fucking hell, that could take hours.

My breathing grew labored quicker this round, but I enjoyed it more. The knot of unease was gone, and I was able to appreciate the burn in my muscles.

After a few laps in the park, we were ready to head home again—with just one detour, to pick up overpriced cupcakes.

"Don't tell anyone I overreacted before," I said, breathing heavily.

I could still hear myself. *"It never stays that way!"* Christ. As if us having a little bit of filthy fun with people we cared about would escalate into daily orgies and poly houses.

"Don't sweat it," Greer replied. "Just last week, it was me. I met up with Kingsley for a couple beers after work and spent the whole fuckin' time bitching about getting old. I mean, we have Corey now. A fuckin' twenty-four-year-old. I gotta stay in shape so I can keep up with him."

Boy, did I know the feeling.

3.

I couldn't lie—the run had put me in a great mood. My shoulders didn't feel stiff, my mind was at ease, and I felt reenergized. Not to mention starving. So after a shower and pulling on a pair of jeans and a tee, I headed downstairs and joined the others in the kitchen.

Fuck, everything smelled so damn good this time of year.

"Daddy, I think I need more green," Corey said.

"I'm shocked, really, that you need more of the color of frogs." Sloan had little Kyla on his hip and a smile on his face.

Greer hadn't made it back down yet. But considering Archie was helping him in the shower, who knew how long they'd be.

"Come sit, sweetheart," Luke said. "I'll make you some breakfast."

"Thanks." I grabbed one of the stools and peered over Kit's shoulder to see what they were doing. Safe to say, you could tell one of the boys made a living as an illustrator.

Kit's decorated cookies were still perfect, though. And I said that both as a biased Daddy and someone who'd spent hours next to him on the third floor. His model craft were stunning. He had an eye for detail.

"Lookin' good, boys." I brought the stool to the other side of the island where I wouldn't be in the way.

I wasn't at all surprised to see a color map from his hobby room next to Kit. He'd been mixing icing like a champ, the colors varying from NATO green to desert sand.

Both boys were wearing pajamas and matching expressions of concentration, and for some mysterious reason, they had icing around their mouths.

"Did you hear about Tate's prank for Master Kingsley?" Corey asked quietly.

"Oh my God, I know," Kit replied just as quietly. "He was gonna put it in his stocking, right?"

I cocked my head.

"Yeah." Corey finished applying icing to another cookie and slid it onto a tray at the center of the island. "And then Shay's Secret Santa gift to—you know what I mean."

The boys snickered and sent me a couple furtive glances.

I kept my smirk on the inside.

Luke gave me a coffee mug. "Regression and brat scheming isn't the best combination."

Ha! I'll say.

The boys were cute as fuck, but they couldn't fool anyone if they were in the middle of regressing for our day together. At that point, hide-and-seek would involve a round of peekaboo under the "if I can't see you, you can't see me" premise.

"Ba-ba-ba!" The toddler provided her input too.

Corey looked up from his work and grinned at the girl. "Your daddies will be here soon, Kyla."

That made Kyla laugh.

Babies...

I took a sip of my coffee and reached out, poking the little girl's chubby cheek. Best fucking thing about those little ones, wasn't it? The thick thighs and chubby cheeks. With that said, my sister had never appreciated my calling my niece chunky monkey.

The girl stared at me.

"What did he do, sweetie?" Sloan smiled.

"C'mere," I said. "Lemme get acquainted with our li'l mascot."

"Kids love Daddy," Kit supplied helpfully.

"Everybody loves me, little darlin'." I accepted the chunky monkey into my arms and kissed her cheek. "Hey, you. Maybe you can tell my baby sister to hurry up on cookin' her bun."

Kyla babbled excitedly and gestured between the boys and me.

In the meantime, Sloan rounded the island to help Corey mix more icing, and yeah, maybe I checked out his ass a little bit. Kit was onto something. Luke and Sloan shared a few features. Maybe Sloan was more rough around the edges. He had the rocker vibe going with tats and piercings.

The kitchen filled with the smell of eggs and bacon, and my stomach rumbled with hunger. At the same time, Kyla started bouncing on my thighs as a new Christmas song began playing in the background.

"Aw, you like the country Christmas music too, don't you?" I poked her nose. "That's a good girl. Yeah, it's a great tune, innit?"

It was a good time to hear Greer and Archie coming down the stairs because my breakfast was almost done.

Their arrival set the kitchen in motion for a couple minutes, where everyone was talking at once. Greer stole the girl from me, Archie snuggled up with Sloan and promised Corey to keep an eye out for something he wanted for snacks later, Kit threw a hissy fit when he didn't get the jet design right on the cookie, Luke served me my breakfast, and then the doorbell rang.

I shut it all out and ate in silence. Bacon was perfect, eggs were perfect, coffee was even better.

"Is that Reese, Daddy?" Kit demanded.

That was a Luke-Daddy. Not a Colt-Daddy.

"I don't know. Go see, please," Luke replied.

"It could be my sister," Archie said. He'd taken over Kyla by now, and they were on their way out. "Okay, just remember, dinner at Corey's place at six—"

"We agreed to call it our city place, Archie!" Corey complained. "Since you shut down the Game Cave idea that Jason and I had."

Greer chuckled and kissed the top of Corey's head.

"We're not calling our second home the *Game Cave*," Archie grated out. "Bloody hell, it's bad enough we eat so much takeout there."

I grinned around a mouthful of bacon. It was an interesting dynamic, that one. To my understanding, Greer's farmhouse outside of Winchester was their primary home, but since Sloan's kids weren't starting school out there till after the holidays, they had frequent sleepovers at Corey's condo in Arlington, which was just a few blocks away from the kids' schools and day care.

"Excuse me for not prioritizing a big kitchen when I bought the place for myself, a single, little person." Corey rolled his eyes.

"You're excused, my love." Archie finished the conversation with a kiss to Corey's cheek and a, "Have fun today, guys. And I'll see you again tomorrow, Kit."

"Yeah, okay—bye, Archie!" Kit waved. "Thank you for bringing the cookies!"

Greer walked them out, and I assumed it wasn't Reese at the door since nobody came in.

"Can I just say, Archie's eyes are like freakin' stunning?" Kit said quietly.

"I know, right?" Corey was in total agreement. "It's like, you look at him and can't look away. Even when he's being a poophead."

I smirked into my coffee mug and finished the last of it.

Our boy was sure as shit having himself a gander.

But after my run with Greer, something had changed within me. I started seeing possibilities instead of worries. And it made sense, I reckoned. I had to go through the worry phase first. Luke had pointed out more than once that when I had something to lose, I tightened my hold before I could be talked into relaxing. I'd done the same with him.

I caught Sloan and Luke chuckling about something together in the corner. Scheming Daddies and scheming brats? Or maybe Luke and Sloan were just getting to know each other better. They sure looked chummy.

Feeling the need to clear my head, I grabbed Greer as soon as he returned. We had work to do. Luke's list was miles long.

"Don't forget to hang the mistletoe, Daddy!" Kit said.

Right. Mistletoe. Of course.

Over the next couple of hours, we ticked items off the list one by one. Mistletoe up—in the doorway between the kitchen and living room. All the Christmas decorations boxes went up in the attic. A pot on the stoop for the smokers tomorrow. Readying the beds in the guest rooms. Checking inventory for the bathrooms, resulting in Greer stepping out to buy more toilet paper. In the meantime, I gathered the china we'd use for the buffet and stacked everything on the table in the dining room. Then Reese stopped by with a big box filled with Band-Aids.

"You wanna come in for coffee?" I asked.

"Would if I could, but I'm meeting up with Shay in twenty."

He handed over the box. "Fourth mission to find River something for Christmas. He's fuckin' impossible to shop for."

I grinned. "What's wrong with a year's supply of ramen cups?"

He offered a flat look. "Everything. Fucking everything, Colt."

I laughed and set the box on the floor.

"What did you get Luke?" he asked under his breath.

"He's easy, I'm afraid. Couple nice shirts, a new Kindle, and a pair of leather shoes he's been eyein' for months."

They'd cost a pretty penny.

Reese sucked his teeth and ran a hand through his hair.

"You're buildin' a new house next year," I pointed out. "What about somethin' for that?"

"Reese, is that you?" Luke called from the kitchen.

"Yeah—sorry, I can't stay, hon," Reese called back. Then he turned his attention back to me and said, "We'll think of something." He pointed to the box next. "You mind putting your boy to work?"

"Not at all," I assured. "I know the drill."

"Perfect." He gave my arm a squeeze and opened the front door again. "See you tomorrow—and thanks for letting us snatch one of the guest rooms."

"'S'what they're here for, buddy. See you tomorrow."

I closed and locked the door, then carried the big box into the kitchen. Kit and Corey were still at it, but I could tell the excitement had worn off. They must've decorated over a hundred cookies by now.

"I have a new project for you when you're done here, boys," I told them.

Corey gasped. "Is that the annual Band-Aid supply?"

"That's right, son. It'll be Kit's first year, so I'm sorry to spoil the surprise, baby." I placed the box on an empty stool and flipped it open. Countless packets of Band-Aids, plain ones and kid-themed ones, filled the box—along with small cellophane bags and greeting cards from the twins.

Kit sucked an icing-coated finger into his mouth and peered into the box. "So is that the Tenleys' Secret Santa gift or something?"

"No, it's unrelated," I replied.

"They give the masos a packet of Band-Aids every Christmas," Corey explained. "Last year, I got five *Star Wars* Band-Aids!"

Kit grinned and scrunched his nose. "A weekend supply, then."

I chuckled. "You'll be sortin' all these once you're finished here. Five in each bag, with a card."

It was River and Reese's way of wishing everyone a merry Christmas.

"Okay, Daddy," Kit replied.

"Will do, Sir," Corey chimed in. "Beats sorting through Mclean House propaganda."

"Hey, now." I ruffled his hair.

"Colt, may I have a word...?" Luke nodded toward the doorway.

I inclined my head and followed him out.

...and up the stairs, apparently. He wanted privacy for whatever he was going to say.

In one of the guest rooms, he sat down on the side of the bed and patted the spot next to him.

"Am I in trouble?" I smiled.

He smirked a little but said nothing—until I sat down.

"Are you okay?" He shifted toward me and pulled one leg up on the mattress. "You've been broody all morning."

Broody? My eyebrows hitched reflexively. Maybe I'd come off as broody, but... "No, I've just had a bit on my mind." And I might as well fess up. "I think Kit's ready to explore group play, so I wanna prepare myself. Rewire my brain a little."

Luke wasn't surprised. We'd touched on this before.

"Why would you need rewiring?" he wondered. "We've enjoyed some group play before."

Hence the need. "That's the thing, innit? I was more relaxed before we met Kit. Now I'm stompin' around to protect my territory, and that's no way to live."

Luke grinned faintly and pressed a kiss to my shoulder. "Don't be too hard on yourself. We're not as open as many of the others, and that has nothing to do with us being territorial."

That was true, but I had limits. "Still. I've made the leash too short. While you'll never find me at one of Mack's events, or including others in our relationship, I wanna explore those dirty playdates we used to talk about."

I just hoped...Kit wouldn't venture too far outside our triad.

Luke gave me a warm, lazy little smile and a quick kiss.

While I was at it, I offered a recap of my run with Greer and what we'd discussed. From various scenarios to personal limits. I had no problems with Luke playing with others as long as I was present, be it a Little or a Top. For myself, I didn't wanna be too intimate with a Little. If we were to play with Greer's crowd, I was more likely to see if I could make Sloan bend over, something that made Luke chuckle as he kissed my jaw.

That was a fictive example, though. Sloan stuck to Archie and Corey, which was fine. We hadn't decided anything yet.

As for Kit...

"Are you listenin' to me?" I had to ask. 'Cause he wouldn't stop smooching my face.

"Of course I am." He cupped my cheek and kissed the other. "Some of us can multitask. I can listen to you, kiss you, and fantasize about you prancing around naked in Florida at the same time."

I snorted. I didn't fucking prance. But yeah, considering Ty's house was in the Ten Thousand Islands south of Naples, we'd been promised secluded mangrove islands where clothes were optional. Luke was *really* looking forward to a vacation in the sun. He'd started packing and everything.

"You were going to say something about Kit," he said.

Right.

I cleared my throat and tried to focus, even as his hand landed on my crotch. "I'm gonna push for us to be able to vet whoever he wants to play with. As his Owners, I think that's our right. He's still new, and his eyes are bigger than his stomach at times."

"Agreed." He grazed his teeth along the shell of my ear, causing me to shudder. "I don't think he's particularly interested in playing with Tops, just so you know. Corey and Kit spent an hour downstairs discussing who the best kisser among the subs might be. They both put their money on Macklin because he has—and I quote—so much experience, and he's like the hot big brother you dream about."

"Jesus," I exhaled in a laugh. "We'll tell Mack tomorrow. He loves to make boys blush."

If Kit mostly wanted to explore with Littles, I'd be able to relax fully. And if he didn't...if he wanted to play with other Daddies—well, I'd cross that bridge then. I didn't wanna think about it.

That night after dinner, I *wanted* to enjoy myself the way Kit and Luke were clearly doing. Well, after some minor drama with the most stubborn housekeeper I'd ever met.

She'd been downstairs all day, and she'd been offended when we had wanted to pay her extra for her work. My fucking

God, the woman had a colorful vocabulary. I didn't need to know Spanish to understand I was now her enemy. And the *gestures*... But according to her, this party, all the cooking, was her way to thank us for making her retirement bearable. Her words, not mine. But the joke was on her, because we'd just give her more money for groceries to use when volunteering at her church. She may be headstrong, but I wasn't born yesterday, and I had a Kit with puppy-dog eyes. I wasn't afraid to use him.

After she'd gone home, however... Smooth sailing. We'd had dinner. We'd finished everything we had on our lists for the day. So now, Kit and Luke were bringing cupcakes and coffee—cocoa for the boy—into the living room to watch another Christmas movie.

I had this rock in the pit of my gut that wouldn't dissolve, but I went through the motions anyway.

"Did you read Cam's latest journal entry, dear?" Luke asked. "His and Lucian's journey is so beautiful."

Kit snickered and sat down on the couch. "I kinda liked Noa's entry more. I *howled*, Daddy."

My mouth twitched. Of course he preferred Noa's entry. Cam wrote in great detail about servitude and how his slave training impacted him, and Noa did...not. Sometimes the boy got good-naturedly jealous of the attention Cam's entries received online, so Noa was now spitting out journal entries every day.

Today's entry read, "Just had an excellent poop!"

I joined Luke and Kit with my own coffee and a better snack and sat down in the corner of the sectional. The very spot I'd held Kit for the first time. It was mine. This was where I napped, where I watched the news, and where I could look out over the rest of the living room and dining room.

"Is that the thing from Alaska, Daddy?" Kit asked. "From your Air Force buddy?"

"Well, his brother. He's a helicopter pilot with the Coast Guard up there. And every year, he sends jerky to Andy, who ships some of it to me." I unwrapped the piece of jerky, then placed it on the little cutting board I'd brought. Caribou jerky straight from Alaska beat overpriced cupcakes any day of the week. "You'll meet Andy at Miramar next year," I said. Miramar would be the first air show I attended with Kit, and I knew exactly what I was looking forward to the most. Just seeing his reactions to the displays.

"Oh! Is he flying there?" Kit asked.

I nodded and carved a slice of jerky with my folding knife. "He just joined the C-17 demo team on the West Coast."

Kit dropped his jaw. "Oh. My. God."

I grinned and chewed on the best jerky a man could ask for. Christ, every Christmas—it was one of the best gifts. Smoky-sweet, with a generous dose of big game.

I wondered how Kit would react the day I told him he'd get to fly with Andy at Miramar. Luke had declined, stating he only flew planes with drink service, so he'd be on the ground while Kit and I watched a couple dozen paratroopers jump out of a C-17.

"Pop quiz," I said abruptly. "What's the wingspan of a C-17?"

Kit shot straight up and didn't miss a beat. "It's 169 feet and ten inches, Sir!"

Christ almighty, my little geek. I chuckled and took him at his word. Fuck if I knew. I could ramble specs about my Viper in my sleep, but that was about it. I was fairly good with the Eagle and the Raptor too.

Luke tugged on Kit's pajama bottoms. "You're quite the encyclopedia, young sir. Sit down and eat your cupcake. We don't need more frosting on this couch."

Kit snickered and plopped back down, and he carefully

peeled down the wrapper on his cupcake before he bit into the top with an audible "owrrmph."

I couldn't describe with words how fucking cute he was.

My chest swelled and tightened uncomfortably, the irrational worries intensifying. What if he did want to play with other Tops? What if he began hungering for arrangements and dynamics outside what we had? We wouldn't exactly be able to blame him for it. He was so young.

If I considered how many times I'd changed my mind about relationships at that age... On the other hand, I'd always been monogamous. Commitment was another matter. At twenty-two, I'd fucked my way through the gay population of every Air Force town I'd lived in—twice. It wasn't until I hit thirty that I'd had my first real relationship.

Luke was my first forever. Just like I was his.

Kit was supposed to be our second and last.

I was losing it. Halfway into the holiday flick, I couldn't even say what it was about.

Whenever Kit gigglesnorted and laughed, I had to refocus and refix my gaze on the screen. Elves were running around, Vince Vaughn was handsome as usual, and Santa couldn't deliver gifts on time.

Luke kept glancing my way, and I didn't know what to do. I knew I was being obvious to him. For one, I wasn't lying down like I usually did when it was movie time. For two, I was squeezing the shit out of a stress toy Kit had given me just the other week. The boy had noted I got stressed out from work sometimes, so he'd spent "all the quarters" to win a stress toy shaped like a baby shark from a gumball machine for me. How fucking sweet was that?

The toy sure saw action too. Less when I was stressed, more when I was irrationally worried about my boy running off with another Daddy Dom.

The whole thing was ridiculous. I didn't need Luke or Greer reminding me. But for the sake of argument, who might Kit be interested in? Greer was a nonissue. We had trust, friendship, chemistry, experience, and attraction. He and Kit together wouldn't worry me much—despite how I'd behaved this morning. I'd let that go. We could easily go the playdate route and have fun together, with the boys at the center of our attention. And then what? Or *who?* KC? Beau? Nathan? How was I gonna stomach that?

"I think this is a good spot to take a little break," I heard Luke say. His words pulled me back to the present, and I reckoned he was going to the bathroom. "We should talk a bit about expectations for tomorrow before we get too tired." He pressed pause on the movie.

So no bathroom break?

"I expect to have fun!" Kit grinned and crawled up on Luke's lap. "What else is there to talk about?"

Luke chuckled and combed his fingers through the boy's messy hair. "How about playtime?"

Kit perked up.

I frowned.

"We're gonna play tomorrow?" Kit asked.

"Yeah, are we?" I wondered.

Luke gave me a pointed look. "I think that's a fair assumption when you put twenty kinksters in a room with alcohol and merciless teasing between Sadists and brats."

"The Sadists are worse," Kit insisted. "We're innocent."

I wasn't gonna dignify that with a response.

Luke didn't take the bait either. "Will you be innocent under the mistletoe as well, little one?"

Aw, hell. He was gonna broach the topic I was hoping to avoid, and he was doing it via the mistletoe discussion. Which wasn't so much a discussion as it was a quick mention and a note with limits.

Kit eyed the mistletoe hanging in the kitchen doorway, then glanced back at Luke. He wasn't our little clown at the moment. His mind was racing.

"I don't know what you mean, Daddy."

I cleared my throat, figuring I could take this one and then Luke could handle the rest. "We've had a mistletoe tradition out in Mclean the past few years—and there ain't a whole lot to discuss. If you happen to run into a Top under the mistletoe, he's allowed to be a nice Sadist to you."

"Nice Sadist!" Kit laughed. "Ain't no such thing, sugar."

I smiled.

"You do have options, though," Luke elaborated. "First of all, we're talking about a few seconds. No one is taking their clothes off or racking up a collection of bruises in the doorway."

Kit scrunched his nose and grinned a little. "See, I thought it was just a sweet thing between partners. Like, if you and I walk under the mistletoe at the same time, we kiss. But if I walk under there with Master Kingsley, nothing happens."

Sweet, sweet, innocent mind. How I adored him.

"That's one of the options." Luke's eyes flashed with mirth. "I, for one, don't normally partake in the game. It's totally up to you."

That caused Kit to shift his gaze to me, and the question was written on his face.

"Of course I'm joinin'." I hadn't missed a year. "It's my annual wrist exercise." I flexed my hand as if I was ready to smack a nice little ass. Which was essentially what I'd done the previous mistletoe years. Three quick whacks got any party started.

Kit snickered. "I think you've gotten plenty of exercise on my butt too."

"And that's another option." Luke cut in again. "If you join the game, you choose the body parts the Top can do something to, and some opt for the butt. But you can choose arms, thighs, nipples, hair, mouth—"

"Mouth!" Kit squeaked. "I don't want to get smacked in the mouth!"

Christ, he was so innocent. Despite the tightness in my gut, because I sensed Luke was slowly getting closer to the topic he was aiming for, Kit's expressions were like aloe on a sunburn.

"Mouths are usually for kissing." There we go. Luke had gone there now. The door was open. "In short, you write down your limits on a note, and those limits apply to every Top who will be here. If kissing is okay, you can add mouth to the list."

Even in the dim lighting from the TV and the Christmas tree, I saw the blush creeping forward on Kit's face.

"No one's gonna stick their tongue down your throat, baby," I said. I didn't want him to overthink this tradition. It was just a fun little game running in the background. "Tate, for instance, will write somethin' like, *just go for it*, because he knows nobody will take anythin' very far. It's a smack here, a smooch there, and maybe a quick tug on his hair to piss him off. Cam, on the other hand—if he's allowed to join—might write down ass and thighs. Tops will stay away from the rest of him, and we'll give him a spank or two in passing. But I reckon most of the subs will write similarly to Tate."

"Which is easier for all the Tops to remember," Luke chuckled.

I grinned. That was true.

Kit snuck an arm around Luke's neck and seemed to hesitate. "What happens when Tops meet each other in the doorway, then? Or two bottoms?"

I shrugged. "Nothing."

"Laaaaame." He grinned, but something was missing in his eyes. He was uncertain—maybe. Either way, it brought out my protectiveness in full force, because the last thing I wanted him to feel was uncertain. "It's much funner when two Daddies kiss and stuff."

Hmm. He'd said something to that effect before.

"There will probably be some of that too, sweetheart," Luke assured. "You haven't witnessed Reese and Colt drunk yet."

I snorted under my breath and rolled the stress toy between my hands. I was changing my mind. It would've been comfortable to stick my head in the sand a few more days, but if Luke was insisting on discussing potential group play, we might as well cut the shit and speak bluntly. I couldn't sit here and watch him slowly peel off the Band-Aid.

"It's better we discuss who Kit wants to make kissy faces with." To use his brat terminology. "You've been on and on about Greer and me, so how about you with others? Is that somethin' you're curious about? Or, you know, playin' with others in general." I cleared my throat and went a step further to eliminate his potential worry of giving the "wrong answer." Because I knew Kit. "Wantin' to explore with others is perfectly natural."

"Absolutely," Luke agreed. "Colt and I are a little curious about your thoughts on this—on group play and so on. We have a lot of that in our community."

Too much of it, one part of me wanted to say. And then Luke would accuse me of bitching.

Fuck giving him the satisfaction of being right.

Kit had suddenly turned into ten shades of shy, all but hiding his face against Luke's neck, so it was safe to say he had opinions on the matter.

"You're not on trial here, little darlin'. Whatever you say and feel is okay."

He bit his lip and refused to make eye contact. But a beat later, he crawled off Luke's lap and bolted for my lap instead, where he locked his arms around my neck and whispered in my ear.

"Maybe I want to play with Corey."

I exhaled a laugh and squeezed him to me. It was fucking insane how relief and worry could simultaneously fuck with my body. My shoulders felt stiff, my heart beat a little faster, emotions rumbled like thunder. Corey was another nonissue. Most subs were. It would be cute and hot as fuck to see them play together.

"Daddy and I kinda figured you had a little crush on Corey." I kissed the side of his head and tossed the stress toy onto the coffee table. "Who else?"

"Umm..." He fiddled with the neckline of my tee. "Maybe Macklin. He's like a dirty big brother. And he's so hot."

Yeah, I could definitely see that. Macklin would shoulder that role perfectly for Kit.

Luke shifted closer and gathered Kit's legs on his lap.

So far, so good.

Then Luke had to ask the question with the answer I dreaded. "Are there any Tops and Daddies you'd like to play with?"

I swallowed hard and had to force myself not to go rigid. Whatever the answer, we could work it out together. I had to believe that.

Kit sat up a little straighter so he could see Luke too, and he scrunched his nose in thought. "Not really. I'm more into the live porn, you see?"

I coughed a laugh; my ears were fucking ringing all of a sudden, and I could hear my own pulse. The boy had my goddamn sanity in his grip. Could I relax yet? I wasn't sure. I didn't think so. He wasn't done.

"Okay, I think Greer is super-duper hot," he admitted. "He has a way about him, and it would be sexy to maybe do something with him and Corey—like, all of us together. Something milder. I'm not as uninhibited as, you know, Corey or Noa. I don't want to go the whole way or play without limits."

Everybody had limits, but I got what he was saying, and hope exploded within me. The sensation was so forceful that I gusted out a breath and had to mask my relief with another cough.

"What would you like to do, then?" Luke asked. "Say we put together a playdate—the three of us with Greer and Corey."

"Oh, I don't knowww." Kit groaned and fell against me again, and I squeezed him tightly to me. "Daddy put all these fantasies in my head. I'm innocent!"

So he kept saying.

"It would be hot to see Colt and Greer fuck Lucas," the boy confessed in a rush. "Cuz that's what happened way back in the day when you were young."

I rumbled a laugh as the relief poured out of me.

Meanwhile, Luke got offended. "When we *were* young? Boy, I'm still young."

"You know what I mean!" Kit giggled. "That's what turns me on, though. To see Tops together. Maybe it would be exciting and hot to kiss Greer a little...? I even made a list of friends I would deem safe to play with, but that doesn't mean I'm interested. Or—I mean, it doesn't mean they're interested or available either. Like with Cam. He would be safe. Tate also. But..." He trailed off, and so did the amusement. He hesitated again. "Thing is... I don't want to get very intimate with another Daddy or regular Dom, and I don't want to see my Daddies with other Littles too much. I'm sorry."

I shook my head and gathered his face in my hands, and I couldn't stress this enough, what I was about to say. "You have *nothin'* to apologize for, baby. You got that? Absolutely nothin'. In fact—" I took a deep breath. The relief was still rushing through me. "I've been frettin' my rear off all damn day, thinkin' maybe you wanna explore arrangements with other Daddies— and it's possible I'm a bit possessive of you."

I deserved the look I received. I deserved every ounce of his disbelief and even the sense of "What the fuck, how could you think that of me?" that I detected in his eyes. That was the rational part I'd been trying to summon to cover up the dumbass insecurities I'd suffered from.

"I'm the one who should apologize." I touched his cheek. "Looks like Daddy ain't always so confident."

Luke kissed my shoulder, and Kit's gaze softened a little.

"To each their own, but that's not who I am," he said. "I would like to dip my toe in the water, not jump in. And you know, sometimes the fantasy is meant to stay a fantasy. Imagine if everything we liked in porn became reality!"

He drew a smile from me, to which he grinned triumphantly in return.

"Also," he said, locking his arms around my neck once more, "I like it when you get possessive of me, Daddy. Because the way I see it, it's the three of us against the world forever and ever."

Christ, he fucking owned me.

"Forever and ever sounds perfect to me." I hugged him to me and peppered his face with kisses. "We can dip our toes in that water together."

He nodded and offered a goofy smile that I was all too happy to kiss.

"We'll have a li'l chat with Macklin and Greer, then," I decided. "You just let Daddy and me know how far you wanna go with them. I'm good with whatever you decide where Mack's concerned, and I'm not too worried about Greer and his family either."

Maybe we could plan something for after the holidays.

"And I think I speak for Colt too when I say you're free to flirt with Corey and Macklin," Luke added. "It's always better to let things progress naturally. See if you have chemistry and so on."

"Absolutely." I nodded. "We can decide that right now—playtime is okay with those two. However far you wanna take it. Then we'll set up more structured play when we get together with both Corey and Greer."

Kit bit his lip and tilted his head. "Just like that? Like...I could kiss Corey tomorrow at the party if he showed interest?"

Well, yeah.

"That's our version of how we'd introduce a Little to playing with someone else," Luke offered. "If you would prefer it another way, tell us. We're all ears."

Kit shook his head quickly. "No, I think that's, um... Yeah. But are you okay with this?" He glanced at me, so I figured the question was aimed more to me than Luke.

"I couldn't pick two better boys for you to explore with," I said. Firmly and honestly. "We know Mack so well, and you and Corey have grown close since he got back to the States."

Corey went to visit family all over the world every summer, but as soon as he'd returned, he and Kit had become two peas in a pod.

"Okay, but, um, can you also be close with Macklin?" Kit pressed shyly. "He's not a Little, and you've played with him before, so maybe that could work and we could kiss and play together sometimes? If he wants?"

I had a feeling Macklin would be on board.

"Macklin is a good exception." I nodded. "I wouldn't feel the same desire to limit myself around him."

His eyes lit up, and he hugged me as if I'd just given him the keys to the nearest ice cream shop. Maybe I had, in a way.

"Just remember to be safe," Luke told him. "No unprotected sex outside our relationship."

"Oh my gosh, Daddy, that's embarrassing," Kit complained. He slapped his hands over his face and everything.

I shook my head in amusement. "If you can't talk about sex, you can't have it either."

He better suck it up because the conversation was far from over.

4.

"The day is finally here! The day is finally here! Wake up, Daddies! The day is finally here!"

Fucking hell. I wasn't ready. Instead, I burrowed closer to Luke under the duvet and pressed my morning wood against his ass.

"Don't jump on the bed," Luke grumbled.

"But it's Christmas party time!" Kit argued. "Rosa's already downstairs. She's preparing the turkeys!"

"Kit, I fuckin' swear," I said. "Quit jumpin' on the bed."

The boy huffed and plopped down on his butt. "Why are you being grinches?"

"The sun isn't even up, little one." Luke tried to be patient. "It's going to be a long day. Get all the rest you can."

I kissed his neck and slipped a hand down to hold his cock.

Another hour of dozing on and off and some cuddles would be nice.

Kit still loved to lower the thermostat to the point where Michigan winters seemed warm. I wasn't getting out from under the duvet anytime soon.

"What if I made you breakfast in bed?" Kit wondered. "And coffee? Would that make you happier?"

I was very happy right where I was, but... "That's acceptable." Coffee did sound nice. "Warm up some scones from the freezer."

"Yes!" Kit left us with a victory shout and darted down the stairs.

"My God," Luke mumbled. "Were we ever that energetic?"

Not like that.

"I sure as hell never jumped on the bed." I smiled sleepily, then yawned and stretched out beside him. "Grab some oil, baby."

"Mmm..." He reached for the bottle on the nightstand and made quick work of preparing himself for me.

Then I took our morning cuddle to the next level and buried myself balls deep in his ass.

"Fuck," he exhaled.

I swear.

"I'll never tire of this." I kissed his neck and just let the sensations wash over me. It was everything from the soft, smooth flesh of his cheeks pressed against my upper thighs, to his asshole stretching around my cock. A hot flash of *holy fuck, this is mind-blowingly great* even nine years later. The urgency came and went, depending on mood and whatnot, but those first few seconds after I pushed inside him hadn't changed since we'd met and we'd fucked our way through the night.

In that moment, I could still see us in Richmond. I could see Luke when he entered the bar and stumbled right into a girl who was there with her older brothers. I could almost reach out and grab the attraction I'd been struck by, which hadn't been the first glance at Luke. It'd been when he'd reached his limit. He'd offered to buy the girl a drink as an apology for sending her to the floor, and the brothers had accused him of buying her silence. And right then and there, Luke had stiffened; his jaw had clenched, and he'd been so fed up.

I'd intervened a second later, feeling fucked in the head.

And wondering, who was this rain-soaked pretty boy who was willing to go up against the linebacker-sized Richmond Royalty?

I let out a long breath and stroked his hip, and my mouth never left his shoulder and neck.

"Right there," he murmured. "Stay there."

I couldn't stay completely still, but I could rub up against that spot in quick thrusts where I never pulled out more than a couple inches.

"Jesus, Colt," he groaned. "I almost need to stroke your ego."

I grinned and sucked on his earlobe. At the same time, I wrapped my fingers around his cock and pushed in harder. Then I slowed down but used longer strokes to tease him.

He moaned and began meeting every movement.

"God, I love your cock," he muttered.

Keep talkin', darlin'.

I could only pace myself for so long, though. Sooner rather than later, I withdrew from him and told him to get on all fours for me. I wanted to get us off before we had breakfast trays in bed.

Luke didn't complain. My perfect cock-whore woke up, pushed out his ass for me, and looked at me over his shoulder as I slammed in.

I started fucking him in earnest, my fingers digging into his hips, and the bed creaked with each thrust.

This was heaven. We found our rhythm and let the sounds and the pleasure seduce us. *Fuck.* He got needy too. I loved it. He didn't beg verbally as much as he tried to get impossibly closer and latch on to me. He eased back on my lap, sinking down on my cock with a satisfied moan, and reached back to thread his fingers through my hair.

"You gettin' there, baby?" I planted an openmouthed kiss along his neck as the pressure built up rapidly within me. He stroked himself quickly, and he was so goddamn sexy. "Fuck—clench down like that again."

I was gonna lose it soon.

"So close," he breathed.

Thank fuck.

I pushed him forward once more so I could fuck him faster and chase my orgasm, and I didn't hold back one bit. My man loved being taken by his savage. It was the only pain he was obsessed with, being fucked brutally.

I screwed my eyes shut and ignored my muscles protesting. The pleasure surged through me like fire, and I was right there, seconds away from letting go. His groans grew louder, and each one fueled me.

Then he was gone. He started coming, moaning and panting, and I sent myself off the cliff. It wasn't like him to come on the sheets; he usually came in his hand these days, but I guessed he really needed to let go. I punched into him a few more times and groaned as I emptied my balls in him. Fucking hell, I really needed this too.

And the post-fuck cuddles that were about to follow.

We're on our way. Tied up toes?

I grinned and responded to Reese.

Absofuckinglutely. Spread the word. The brats should arrive in agony. We have spares for y'all, by the way.

It was settled. I pocketed my phone, then jogged down to the second floor and the guest room where Luke and I kept our kink gear in an armoire.

"Colt!" Kit yelled from downstairs. "Can you help me with

my bow tie?"

"Be right there!" I hollered back. In the bottom drawer of the armoire, I sifted through countless bundles of rope until I found a handful of tiny boxes, not much larger than the cap on a soda bottle. I didn't know if everyone attending had their own set, so I might as well bring what we had downstairs.

Kit was waiting for me by the tree in the living room, and he was so fucking cute I couldn't describe it. He was going all out with nice pants, shoes he'd shined himself, white shirt, suspenders, and a dark green bow tie.

"Daddy said we're gonna take a picture by the tree," he told me. He bobbed his head to the Christmas music playing. "He's getting the stand thingy for the camera."

"Copy that." I left the little rope boxes on the coffee table before I joined him. "Our dashin' baby boy. You look exquisite." I adjusted his bow tie so it sat straight.

He beamed up at me. "So do you, Daddy. Oh! You have your Texas tie on!" That was his name for a bolo tie. "Lucas really loves it when we dress up."

I tapped his nose. "That's why we do it." Mostly, anyway. Had it not been for Luke, I would've been satisfied with slacks and one of my nicer pullovers. I wasn't a fan of button-downs unless they came in flannel. But for Luke, I could suck it up with a black shirt and Luke-approved leather shoes. "It's also why we drink."

The boy cracked up hard. "Oh yeah! Can I also get tipsy tonight?"

"Absolutely. I start slingin' cocktails in..." I checked my watch. An hour till five. "One hour."

But first, pictures. Luke joined us with his camera and tripod, lookin' fine as fuck too. He had no issues donning suits.

"My, my, look at you two." He smiled, satisfied, and set up the camera.

I folded up the sleeves of my shirt and did a quick scan of the living room and dining room. All we had left was the food that needed to be reheated. Rosa had left strict instructions before she'd gone home.

"By the way, will I have time to meet up with Vincent before Christmas?" Kit wondered. "He invited me over to check out his new office, and then we wanna do lunch."

"Of course, sweetheart. That sounds fun," Luke replied.

I inclined my head. "You don't have anythin' planned tomorrow or the day after."

"Suh-weet! I'll text him later. I gotta pick up candy too," Kit said. "Just because he's the head of security now does not mean he won't need lollipops and Reese's."

I grinned and shook my head. Maybe Vincent had enjoyed being Kit's overprotective driver before, but the man was thriving at Kit's old man's corporation now. Plus, he and Kit had a much better relationship, and it was fun watching Kit mothering Vincent a little, making sure the man "got enough sugar."

"All right, my loves." Luke was finally ready. "Three pictures in three-second intervals for sixty seconds."

Jesus. "What happened to two shots?"

"Humor me," he said. "In front of the tree, everyone. Kit, you'll stand in front of Daddy and me. Alexa, play 'The Christmas Song' by Thomas Rhett. Colt, no funny business. I truly want a nice family photo out of this."

"Yes, sir—no bunny ears behind Kit's back," I confirmed.

Kit swung an incredulous look my way, before he narrowed his eyes accusingly.

"I said I *wouldn't*," I insisted.

"Yeah, but I don't believe you!"

"That ain't my problem, son," I laughed. "Now, turn around. Let's get these pictures for Daddy so he's happy all night."

He huffed but obeyed, and I threw an arm around Luke's shoulders and kissed his cheek by the first sound of the shutter.

For several seconds, everything went off without a hitch. I was certain Luke was getting his family photo. We smiled for the camera; we showed all the lovey-dovey behavior we had in us, and we complied with every position change Luke demanded. But, then, he'd chosen to spend the rest of his life with a Sadist and a brat. That was his informed decision.

In my defense, Kit started it.

"Alexa, play 'Lit This Year' by Florida Georgia Line!" he called.

"Yee-haw." I nudged Luke and grinned when he sighed heavily and pinched the bridge of his nose. "Aw, come on, darlin'. We gotta have some fun too, don't we?" I couldn't stand his li'l scowl, even less so when Kit began twerking for the camera, so I started moving to the beat and pulled Luke in for a quick twirl. "Wipe that frown off your face and dance with me."

"Yee-haw!" Kit echoed. "We're gonna have so much fun tonight! And my Daddies are gonna kiss all the other Daddies. They promised!"

Had we? I had no recollection of that.

I rumbled a chuckle and nipped playfully at Luke's jaw. He was thawing out—he couldn't help himself. I bobbed my head and sang about Santa getting lit this year, which finally coaxed a sexy grin onto his face.

"Hey, beautiful." I brushed my lips to his. "You know this is how we'll get the best pictures, yeah?"

He offered another sigh, but this one wasn't revealing how insufferable he found us. "Perhaps you're right."

Damn straight.

"Do you know what else my Daddies promised?" Kit demanded.

I smirked and turned to him, and I extended a hand, wanting him with us. "No, what did they promise?"

"I can't dance now. I have ants in my pants!" Instead, he opted to run circles around us, the damn clown. "My Daddies are getting married," he sang. "Colt's gonna wear his formal Air Force mess dress, and they'll walk under the Arch of Sabers after the ceremony, and then three squadrons of fighter jets will roar above in formation, and—"

"Three *squadrons*?" I laughed. "Boy, not even the SecDef would get that treatment."

As a semi-retired colonel, I'd be lucky to get scrap metal from the boneyard in Arizona.

Kit stopped abruptly and stared up at me, hands on his hips. "This is *my* dream, not your—" And that was where the doorbell cut him off. He gasped, and in that split second, his regression was clear as day. "Someone's here already! I'll go see!"

"Look before you open, Kit!" Luke called after him.

"I will!"

I assumed the Tenleys were here, which gave me about five seconds of peace with Luke before the party started.

"By the way, we're doing Tied up Toes." I pressed a quick kiss to his lips.

"Oh—excellent. I thought about that the other day." He slipped his hands to the back of my neck and up into my hair, and I groaned at how good it felt.

Funny, wasn't it, how sometimes a single touch could make you go from alert and ready for a holiday party to wondering why the fuck we didn't take a nap earlier when we'd had the chance between chores.

I needed a drink and a snack.

"Well, rope's on the table." I cleared my throat and shook off the sudden bout of tiredness. "I'mma greet our first guests and throw back a couple shots."

He chuckled and kissed my cheek. "Be careful, baby. We've barely eaten today."

Of course not. I needed room for the Christmas buffet. Two scones for breakfast; other than that... I'd grabbed some snacks in passing.

The cheerful talk in the entryway grew louder, so Luke and I exchanged a last kiss before we shouldered the roles of hosts for the night. And I'll be fucking damned—Kit and Shay were discussing how hot it was for Tops to kiss. Was this a community-wide topic these days? I'd heard it lately from Tate and Corey too.

"Hey—chatterboxes! Lemme through." Reese squeezed by the brats and entered the living room with two big shopping bags.

"Welcome back, buddy. Secret Santa gifts in or around the burlap sack next to the tree." I pointed as I joined him at his side and squeezed his shoulder. It was gonna be a pornographic night for my man, who appreciated everyone dressing up. "Snacks and alcohol on the buffet table." I gestured to the setup next to the dining room table. Too small to hold a dinner for twenty people, but perfect for drinks. "And your guest room is the second door to the right on the second floor."

"Fuckin' A, this is fantastic. Shay! Kit, you too—unless..." He turned back to me. "Did you tie him up yet?"

"I was just about to," Luke said. He'd spotted the rope boxes on the table. "Shay, you can bring your shoes. Just wipe them off on the doormat first. Then you can come over here. You as well, Kit. Shoes and socks off."

"Socks...?" Kit looked puzzled.

"That's what I said, little one." Luke nodded. Then he leaned to the side a bit and said, "Hello, Shay, I forgot to say."

Shay smiled politely. "Hi, Sir. Man, it smells good in here." He smiled at me too. "Thanks for having us, Sir."

"Our pleasure, pet."

River joined us last, carrying a duffel bag.

"Wait—fuck." Shay shifted where he stood, pushing up the sleeves of his shirt. "Is this the infamous tying toes or whatever? Tate told me about it."

I smirked.

"Tied up Toes," Reese corrected. "You obey Colt and Lucas now, you hear? Riv and I will get us settled upstairs."

I clapped Reese on his back. "I'll make you a couple drinks in the meantime."

"Wonderful. For the record, Shay's limits for the mistletoe game are whatever floats your boat, just stay away from his ass. We bruised it pretty bad yesterday."

"Pretty bad?" Shay retorted incredulously. "My entire ass is *black*."

"Oof." I smiled widely. "Some nice deep-tissue bruises then, huh?"

"It's fuckin' incredible—I'll show you later," Reese promised. I was looking forward to that. "First he came so hard that he lost his breath, and then he cried so hard that he lost the spaghetti dinner he'd had with his brothers on the floor."

I barked out a laugh, having been there. First couple times we did more intense pain play with Kit, he'd thrown up both soda and ice cream.

Kit shot me a scowl but said nothing as he plopped down on the couch and removed his shoes and socks.

The twins took the opportunity to take their things upstairs, except for one of the shopping bags.

After mixing a few strong drinks and filling a small bowl with nuts, chips, crackers, and a thick slice of some French cheese, I returned to the couch with a packed tray and took a seat in the corner.

By then, Luke was wrapping Kit's toes with a thin, three-ply jute rope with pretty rough fibers.

"How bad can it be?" the boy asked.

I chuckled.

Then I threw a couple chips into my mouth and nodded at Shay. "C'mere, boy. Let's get your toes tied up too."

Reluctance rolled off his shoulders as he sat down next to me.

I grabbed one of the rope boxes, then unceremoniously lifted his legs across my lap, causing him to yelp. "So what did Tate say about this wonderful little game?"

"Well, he didn't call it *wonderful*, for starters." Shay adjusted in his seat and leaned back on his hands. He didn't look comfortable one bit, which I assumed had something to do with his bruised ass. "He said it's the type of predicament bondage that slowly drives you fucking insane until you're ready to sell your soul for a break."

Luke and I chuckled.

"But it's just soft rope between the toesies...?" Kit didn't get it yet. Bless him.

Shay's foot twitched as I began circling the thin rope around his toes. Over and under, over and under, over and around. Rinse and repeat, back and forth.

River and Reese returned when I was halfway done, and they helped themselves to the drinks I'd mixed on the tray.

"Plenty of snacks over there too." I nodded toward the living room. "I think Luke hit up every cheese store in DC."

"Cheese is good." River turned and headed off.

"For the record, Kit has similar limits to Shay tonight," Luke mentioned. "Colt and I only ask that no one punctures his skin."

Correct. Our boy had a strict plan to make sure his skin remained hydrated. After the accident and all those months of recovering, laser treatments, skin transplants, he still had to use special lotions and fat creams on a daily basis. It was why I wouldn't let just anybody beat him. The spot mattered, the implement mattered, the force mattered.

"No worries, little one," Reese said. "I'll be on CBT Express duty tonight. I've been practicin' my grip all day."

"Lord—Luke, you're gonna have to set up the camera to catch everythin' in the doorway," I said.

Luke snorted softly. "It's not a video camera."

It fucking should be.

Kit squeaked. "Wait, isn't CBT cock and ball torture?"

"You catch on quick." I nodded. One last over-and-under, and then I was done with Shay's right foot. "Only one to go, sweetheart. You can put your sock and shoe on this one."

"That's gonna press my toes together," he argued.

"You catch on quick too." I bobbed my head to the beat of the Christmas tune in the background.

Reese merely grinned and took a swig of his cinnamon whiskey drink.

An hour later, we were just waiting for Gael and Macklin. Luke and I had moved out into the kitchen to follow Rosa's instructions, and Lucian and Greer had offered up their slaves to assist us in the kitchen in the basement. So that was where Archie and Cam were currently keeping an eye on the first turkey and a few of the smaller dishes.

I popped open a window and took a swig of my beer, then turned on all the hot plates on the kitchen island. Luke whipped the mashed potatoes a bit more and added butter, and in the meantime, we had Kingsley and KC telling us their subs' reactions to Tied up Toes.

As a reaction whore, I appreciated this a whole lot.

To no one's surprise, Noa complained the loudest about his itchy toes. Tate was bitching and trying to stay still in the living room.

Speak of the devil...

Noa poked his head into the kitchen and glared at us. "I will fuck you up for this, Daddy!"

KC threw a disinterested glance at his boy. "Oh, will you?"

I snorted. "We already know you're all hat and no cattle, little one. No need to make it any clearer."

"What does that even mean?" the boy demanded. "I'm suffering here! My shoes were already tight!"

"You should've thought about that," Kingsley noted.

Noa let out a frustrated growl and turned away again, only to walk right into a smirking River. Under the mistletoe.

"For fuck's sake!" Noa cried out.

I laughed.

"Fancy meetin' you here, brat." River wasted no time. He trapped Noa against the doorframe in a chokehold and then—oh hell, he stepped on Noa's feet. "Has your Daddy ever mentioned it's nice hearin' you scream?"

That's exactly what Noa did. "Shut up, you gorilla! That fucking hurts! Oww!"

River chuckled and finished up with a kiss to the top of Noa's head. "Go cry somewhere."

KC grinned in satisfaction and finished his drink. "All right, I think I need to go sit down."

"That's what I've been telling you!" Lucian called from the living room.

Those two made me smile. Ever since coming out as a dynamic of four, Lucian and KC, childhood friends, had turned into one of those old married couples, where Lucian was the one constantly fretting over KC.

"Daddy!" Kit yelled from somewhere. "I think Macklin is

here! Yes, that's him! I see him outside the window!"

"Excited much?" Shay teased.

"Um, yeah." If blushing could be transferred to tone, Kit nailed it. "Why are you looking at me like that, Franklin? Stop analyzing me, please!"

"He's probably just horny," Noa said.

"For heaven's sake," Franklin grated out.

I chuckled and pressed a kiss to Luke's cheek on my way out of the kitchen. Jack and Franklin were cozying up on the couch next to River and Shay. Reese and Sloan were checking out my record collection, Kit was on his knees on the couch, peering out the window like an exuberant puppy, and I assumed Greer and Corey were in the basement—never mind. They were raiding the snack buffet with Lucian.

"Are you sure there's nothing we can do to help, Colt?" Jack asked.

"Nah, you sit tight. We're ahead of schedule and everythin'." I ducked out into the entryway and opened the door right before Macklin could knock. And the sight sure was something. "Who died, sweetheart?" Because he looked like someone had died.

"Don't get me started." He kicked snow off his boots and entered, setting a bag on the floor.

I actually would "get started" because he wasn't feeling well, that was for fucking sure.

"Don't take off your shoes yet," I said. Then I hollered for Luke and said Mack and I were gonna check on the slaves in the basement. I pulled on my coat and ushered Mack outside again.

Ahhh, fresh, frigid air. I needed that after the heat in the kitchen.

The private entrance to the studio apartment below was mere feet away, but it'd be a while before we got there.

"Okay, tell me what's wrong."

He shuddered at the cold and glanced at me sideways. "You

always have to push, don't you?"

He knew the answer to that.

If no one pushed, Mack didn't speak. For always wanting everyone else to feel good, he wasn't great at giving himself the same treatment.

He sighed and sniffled, his nose a bit red from the December weather. "I slept with Dean last night."

Jesus Christ.

Yeah, I'd imagine Mack would feel bad about that, seeing as Dean was his brother-in-law. In Mack's defense, he and Walker had been separated for four or five years—four, it had to be four.

Dean had just returned to us after teaching a couple semesters at Stanford. And apparently he'd reconnected with Macklin in a whole new way.

"Well..." I cleared my throat. "What's his take on this whole thing? Y'all didn't technically do anythin' wrong."

"I didn't exactly stick around to find out," Macklin muttered. "It was a drunken mistake."

I nodded. "On account of you still bein' in love with your husband."

That earned me a swift scowl. "I'm not in love with Walker."

I grinned. "All right."

He was in love with Walker. Four years, they'd been split up. And neither could move on. Both had gone through a few relationships since then, each one failing because they couldn't let go of each other.

"By the way, Gael isn't coming," he said. "He stopped by with the Secret Santa gift for Sloan when I was getting ready. He said he wasn't feeling good."

I'd love to say I was shocked.

"That boy's gonna alienate himself sooner rather than later," I murmured. Hell, he was already doing it. "I'll have Luke call him after the holidays." After all, the boy was new in our community. Pushing Macklin, who we'd known well for the better part of a decade, was another matter. If Gael didn't wanna join us, we couldn't force him. "Back to you, pet. How can we turn that frown upside down?"

"My boyfriend's been trying to do that all day."

I lifted my brows. "So you have one of them too?"

Anyone who could keep up with Macklin's love life had to be a stalker.

He nodded with a dip of his chin and shuddered at a harsh gust of wind. "He's amazing. We're open, obviously. Not a single secret between us. But he can't perform miracles."

My mouth twitched with mirth. "Sweetheart, you don't need a miracle. You need your husband."

"For chrissakes, Colt."

I shrugged. "I'm not sayin' you should go back to the monogamous dynamic you had with him before. But don't stand there and tell me you don't miss him."

"You sound like Lane," he bitched under his breath.

"Who's Lane?"

"My boyfriend."

Ah. Well, then. Clever boyfriend. Selfless, too.

"Look." Mack turned to me and took a breath. "What I need tonight is a distraction. Food, way too much to drink, and friends. Maybe I can convince Jack to let me play with him and Franklin too. Lane has a date."

I furrowed my brow. Sometimes I didn't understand him.

"Your last drunken mistake took place *yesterday*—with your brother-in-law—and you're already fixin' to make a new mistake?"

He frowned at me. "Just because I got railed by an orange last night doesn't mean it's a bad idea to sleep with two apples, Sir."

I choked out a laugh, and I had to pull him in for a hug. "You brat. Fair enough." I kissed his temple. "What if you played with two pears and their li'l dragon fruit instead?"

Mack snapped up his head and narrowed his eyes at me.

I smiled.

He really was fucking beautiful, this boy. I'd had a soft spot for Macklin essentially since the day Luke introduced us. Back then, he'd been, what, twenty or twenty-one? Already so certain he was a switch. Already making bold plans to open his own restaurant. And, of course, head over heels in love with Walker.

Just before they'd broken up, Walker had come to me, admitting Luke and I were the only ones he'd like to share Macklin with. But they'd never crossed that line in the end.

"So Kit finally confessed his fantasies," Macklin murmured. "Are you sure it's a good idea to include me? I got the impression he's interested in Greer and you together."

"That too. But he has a crush on you and Corey."

He stood a little taller at that and smiled lazily. "Seriously? He's so goddamn adorable. Count me in for anything that includes you three. Whenever, wherever."

I chuckled and kissed him on the forehead before I eased off. "Always our favorite slut. You can start by flirtin' with him. He's probably too shy to take the first step."

"I'd be happy to," he replied, already looking more upbeat. "So what're the boundaries?"

"You and Kit end up thoroughly fucked." I gave his cheek a light smack and then descended the steps. "He says you're the perfect candidate for a hot, dirty big brother, so…"

"Jesus—I love that boy's mind."

I grinned. So did I. "Come on. We can talk limits while we help Archie and Cam in the basement. Dinner's almost ready."

"Sir, yes, Sir."

5.

We actually managed to squeeze in all nineteen of us around the dining room table that supposedly only seated twelve. Of course, it helped that Noa sat on KC's lap, Corey sat on Greer's, and the Tenley triad shared two chairs.

"Before we dig in!" Luke called out as the last guests took their seats. Good thing we had the buffet set up in the kitchen. It'd be too crowded otherwise. "Colt, Kit, and I just want to say we're so happy you're here. When Kit suggested we host a holiday party, he didn't know we usually have one every year at the house. So it's been a fun month of sharing stories of our traditions—"

"I'd like to scrap the toe bondage tradition!" Kit complained. "My toes hurt so much! And they're sweaty!"

"Sorry, kiddo, we voted on this a couple years ago," Reese said. "Tied up Toes stays."

"Hear, hear." I nodded.

"My Daddy's a lawyer," Noa huffed. "I'll fucking sue."

"You can't afford me, baby boy," KC chuckled.

Several of us cracked up at that. These sweet brats—they'd never cease to make our day.

"It won't be much longer, subbies," Luke assured. "Either

way—it's been fun preparing for tonight, and I hope we can bring some new traditions when we return to our Mclean holiday party next year. Merry Christmas, everyone."

"Merry Christmas!"

"Cheers!"

"Brats rule!"

"Can we eat now, Daddy?" Corey asked.

"Yes, we can eat now," Sloan laughed softly. "Although, I think Reese had something to say too."

"Yeah, but I can talk while you stuff your faces." Reese stood up.

In the meantime, I helped Kit cut his turkey. The food smelled so damn good that my mouth was watering. I'd filled my plate to the max with turkey, ham, ribs, and all the sides we had.

"First of all, thanks for havin' us tonight," Reese said. "Second of all, this isn't a speech so much as it's an announcement. The house is almost ready—at long last. And we've seen the messages online. The rather creative hashtags. #BringBackTheClub, #WeMissYouClubby, #McClubWithdrawals, and so on. So we were thinkin'."

"Don't hurt yourself," Noa blurted out.

I coughed on a piece of turkey, and all the brats laughed with Noa.

"I can't fucking wait to see you under the mistletoe, boy," Reese drawled. "Christ." He shook his head and moved on. "Our first Game of the new year will be called Picture Perfect, and it'll be a little different. For starters, you bring the results to the event. You'll compete in pairs or triads and pick a location, a position, a kink—whathaveyou. You can read all the specifics online starting tomorrow afternoon. And on the night of the event, we'll have a photo exhibit and open up the new and improved Mclean House—shut the fuck up, Noa—with one hell of a club night."

"Fuck yeah!" Tate was on board. He did love a good club night.

"I feel seen," Noa commented somberly.

"We're talking professional DJ and strobe lights that cause seizures," Reese went on, much to the delight of the subs. "We'll have some friends visiting from San Francisco and the Seattle area too, so that'll be fun."

"From Switch?" I asked curiously. Some of our kink furniture came from there. A Daddy Dom had made a name for himself over the years; he was from that community. Excellent woodworker. He'd hit it off with Walker over mutual interests.

"That's the one." Reese nodded to me. "It's a small kink world. We've discovered we have more friends in common out there. Anyway—" He addressed everyone again. "Check out the Game page tomorrow and sign up. Smartphones will work just fine, but we have access to a few proper cameras if any of you need to borrow."

"Oh my gosh, Daddy, we can do our photo shoot in Florida," Kit gushed.

That was a fine idea, actually.

"I hope you'll allow an audience for that shoot," Macklin said.

We'd conveniently seated him on the other side of Kit, and this was why. Our boy flushed and grinned shyly.

"Would you like to watch?"

"Are you kidding me?" Macklin cranked up the predatory oomph in his eyes and snuck in a quick kiss to Kit's cheek. "I'll be in the front row."

Yeah, Kit wasn't gonna stop blushing for a while.

Luke and I exchanged a smirk, and then I gave my food all my attention.

Just a bit more. The third round at the buffet resulted in a smaller plate, but I just needed some more garlic bread, mashed potatoes, and ribs. Luke had picked up some smoked meat that was delicious too.

I stifled a belch as I sat down.

At this point, the only ones still eating were Greer, Reese, Jack, Corey, and me. Kingsley and River were outside smoking —actually, Lucian was missing too. Luke, Archie, Sloan, and Franklin were clearing away plates and preparing coffee.

"Oh, I have one! I have one!" Corey said.

The brats were imitating Sadists...

Corey cleared his throat, all eyes on him, and deepened his voice. "Keep talkin', you're just cruisin' for a bruisin', brat. Keep diggin', keep goin'."

I dropped my fork and stared at the brat.

Kit fucking howled with laughter. "That's my Daddy! Oh my God! That's so Colt!"

Cam laughed too, but he tried to be subtle about it.

Noa never went for subtle. "He's told me that! I've heard him say all those things."

"I have one too." Tate smirked. "Pretend I'm naked—"

"Reese!" every sub yelled.

Okay, that one was hilarious.

Our resident nudist looked up from his plate and went, "Huh?"

I chuckled and shoveled some food into my mouth.

"Is it our turn yet?" Greer drawled.

"Right? I have one," I said with my mouth full. "Pretend my hair's full of products—"

"Tate," Greer and Jack laughed.

Tate folded his arms over his chest and rolled his eyes.

Corey scratched his nose. "Yeah, we're funnier."

"But we can beat you whenever we want," Greer retorted.

"In fact, I propose a spanking competition when we're done here. Anyone game?"

"Absolutely," I said. "I volunteer Luke and Kit." Luke didn't scream Sadist, but he was a fantastic spanko. A real treat to watch.

Kit pointed to himself. "I unvolunteer myself, thank you very much."

How cute he thought that was an option.

"Noa and I are in," KC said. "I think I can speak for Lucian when I say he's in with Cam too."

"But must you?" Cam asked.

I stuck the last of a cheesy garlic roll into my mouth and grinned at their playful, narrowed-eyed exchange. Call me a sap, but I was stoked so many of us had found our kinky love matches this year.

A while later, we were treated to one hell of a show.

Five Doms on the couch, and their subs bare-assed over their laps.

"Owww, Daddy!"

"Jesus fucking Christ!"

"Gah!"

"Ow, ow, ow, ouch!"

Lucian with Cam, Luke with Kit, KC with Noa, Greer with Corey, and Kingsley with Tate.

Just one rule. Be the last brat standing.

Reese and I leaned against the strip of wall between the kitchen doorway and the entryway, drinks in our hands, grins on our faces.

"Come on, Kit! Suck it up!" I hollered.

"What do you think I'm doing?" he groaned. "Ow!"

I took a swig of my drink, appreciating my buddies' different techniques. Greer was the type who let a big paw drop hard, and then he kneaded the flesh of Corey's ass before switching things up with quick, brutal spanks. Kingsley was the Sadist who spread Tate's ass cheeks to get to his asshole too. Lucian had a more sensual approach, but it was no less painful. He alternated between kneading, stroking, and spanking. Luke was somewhat similar, only he focused his pain on a smaller area. Last but not least, KC. A wicked Sadist. Noa couldn't anticipate a single strike, because his Daddy refused to follow a rhythm. One, two, three, one, two, one, two, three, one, one, one, two, three, four. Down to the boy's thighs too.

"Care to make this more interesting?" Jack wondered. "I'll put ten bucks on Corey winning."

Hmm. I turned pensive and eyed the brats. Corey was a good choice. He had a high threshold for pain.

"Ten on Tate," Franklin said.

Another good choice. Tate wasn't a pain slut in that sense, but he had the ability to use pain to gain strength. Pain gave him attitude and made him determined.

"I think Corey too," Reese said.

My gaze landed on Cam. He was the only one who hadn't made a sound yet. Aside from a few gasps and gritty whimpers.

"No bias allowed, gentlemen," Reese added. "If your partner's being spanked, you gotta bet on someone else."

Bless—I loved my boy, I loved how much stronger he'd gotten, but he was no pain slut. Nothing about him was extreme, for which I was thankful. A lower threshold for suffering allowed for fiercer reactions, and those were my crack.

All right, my turn. "I'll put ten on Cam." Because when it came down to it, one thing was stronger than a brat trying to prove a point or being competitive, and that was a slave out to please his Owner.

"My money's on Kit," Sloan said.

"I'm tipsy enough to bet on Noa." River lifted his glass of bourbon. "Cheers."

"I hate you all!" Noa yelled.

"I'll bet on Noa too," Archie said.

"Oh great, a pity bet," Noa groaned. "Jesus, motherfucker, Daddy!"

Shay chuckled. "Sorry, Noa, but my money's on Cam."

I tipped my glass at him. Smart pet.

I glanced at Macklin, who immediately shook his head. "I'm not betting on anyone. Tate's still giving me shit for siding with the Sadists at the boot camp event."

I laughed.

Fair enough.

Over the next several minutes, we got to enjoy five cute asses turning redder and redder. Corey started crying. So did Kit. Tate swore over his Master because "this wasn't the goddamn plan for tonight." The solid smacks filled the air and mingled with the Christmas music in the background. Cam became increasingly upset and couldn't hide the agony he was in any longer. But Tate was the first to safeword.

"Red! Fucking fuck!" He rolled off Kingsley's lap and landed on the floor with a muted thump. "It's supposed to be a party, Master! A vanilla Christmas party!"

Kingsley chuckled and peered down at his boy. "I don't remember seein' vanilla anywhere on the invitation. Come on, sweetheart. Let's go put a cold washcloth on your ass."

Tate whimpered and was dragged off the floor.

"My sweet boy." Kingsley hugged his property to him and kissed the side of his head. "You okay?"

"Jury's still out, Sir," Tate grumbled.

Franklin was frowning. "There's ten dollars I'll never see again. How disappointing."

"Piss off, whore," Tate snapped.

See, that just made Franklin smile. "You say the sweetest things, darling."

Jack cleared his throat. "I'd be careful if I were you, Tate. Next time, I'm the one beating you."

"Shit," Tate muttered.

I shook my head in amusement, then gestured at the guest bath under the stairs. "Have at it. We left plenty of extra towels in there, and there's ice in the kitchen—"

"Oh my God, red!" Corey screamed. Hell, was it really Corey? So soon? "Gah! Fuck! I gotta poop so bad! The. Turkey. Wants. Out." He scrambled off Greer's lap so fast that he nearly tripped, and then he was bolting up the stairs and tugging up his pants. "Daddy, come rub my tummy after, please!"

Sloan was doing his best to keep from laughing. "Of course, baby!"

Maybe I was getting drunk too, 'cause I thought this was too damn funny.

Noa was next to safeword—and the first to stay on his Daddy's lap and cry it out.

Pride swelled in my chest because Kit was a fighter we all underestimated from time to time. But he did throw in the towel a few seconds after Noa, though I was still impressed. And it seemed Shay and I had loot to share when Cam was declared the winner.

"Good job, everyone." I trapped my glass to my chest and gave the boys a round of applause. They'd earned it.

Kit had crawled up to cry it out too, and he clung to Luke like a baby monkey. "C-can we p-please lose the toe bondage now? It itches s-so badly, Daddy."

"We sure can, sweetheart. I'll remove it right now." Luke went all in on the comfort, so I headed over to the snack buffet to mix our boy a drink. He liked it colorful; he liked it sugary sweet.

A nice spanking session tended to have a strong effect on Littles who regressed, and one by one, Kit, Corey, and Noa changed into PJs. They were fucking adorable, cuddled up on the couch, wriggling their freed, chafed little toes, and sniffling and giggling into their cocktails.

It was time for the Secret Santa reveal.

We were prepared.

"Well." Greer slapped his hands against his thighs. "I think I'm gonna step out and buy the paper."

The Littles in the house knew what that meant, and they gasped in delight.

"I'll go with you, Owner," Archie said.

I'd done my part. I'd filled the coffee table with snacks, sweets, and fixings to turn the coffee Irish. I'd also placed more chairs and an ottoman around the table. So I brought a new drink to the couch and squeezed in between Macklin and Reese.

At the same time, Shay came down the stairs after changing into sweatpants and a tee, and I could admit I was a little envious. I loved comfy clothes. But Luke would have my head...

"Come cuddle with Daddy." Reese extended a hand.

Since Kit, Corey, and Noa were busy whispering shenanigans to one another in the corner, I had to use Macklin instead.

I draped an arm around him and sipped from my whiskey. "How are ya, boy?"

He grinned at me. "I'm good, Sir. Are you lit?"

"I'm happy," I corrected. Very happy, in fact. People were having fun. Lucian and Cam were upstairs, and one of them was surely buried in the other. Franklin and Jack shared a spot on the couch and looked lost in their own little bubble. My man was loving the role of party host.

As Shay crawled up on Reese's lap, finding an angle that didn't hurt his bruised ass, River planted himself on the floor between his brother's legs, and soon Shay's fingers found River's hair.

Hell, it wasn't until now I noticed someone had dimmed the lighting. Must've been Luke. I did know he'd lit a bunch of extra candles—and thankfully opened the patio door a sliver.

I removed my tie, noticing several others had done so already. Except for Jack and Franklin, who seemed perfectly comfortable in their suits.

"Luke!" I called. I could hear him chucklin' away in the kitchen with Sloan.

Tate came out from there with a cup of coffee and a smirk. "He and Sloan are busy flirting, Sir."

Perfect. "Then he won't mind I get a little comfortable." I unbuttoned my pants and the top two buttons on my shirt.

"Daddy Lucas!" Kit yelled. "Remember you gots to kiss Tops where we can *see*."

"Jesus Christ, are we still on that?" Reese chuckled. "Shay's fucking obsessed with seeing Daddies and Sadists kiss."

"Because it's fucking hot," Shay replied bluntly.

"Amen!" Kit and Corey chimed in.

I shook my head and finished my whiskey in one swallow. Then I sat back a little lower and let the alcohol sweep through me like a warm wave.

Macklin did the opposite. He sat up straighter and rested his arm along the back of the couch.

"Is there anything I can do for you, Sir?" he asked quietly.

Loaded question. I adjusted my cock and reckoned we had

about ten, fifteen minutes until Santa Greer arrived with his slave helper.

"You can lure Kit over here and pour me another whiskey."

"You can pour me one too, pet," Reese said. "Then you can give Shay a kiss."

"Absolutely, Sir." Mack made quick work of our drinks, and since the boy didn't possess a shred of shyness, he didn't hesitate with the next part. He leaned over me and covered Shay's mouth with his own. All while he slipped a hand between two buttons on my shirt, his fingers teasing my skin.

Yup, that worked, seeing two subbies make out.

I took a sip of my drink and shifted Mack's hand down to my cock to ease some of the pressure building up.

"Yeah, okay, got to go, see you later," I heard Kit say in a rush.

I grinned. In a split-second decision, I decided to give him what he wanted. Right before Kit reached us, I leaned toward Reese and kissed him. A languid, tongue-teasing kiss that was enough to make Kit gasp and whisper, "Oh my goodness."

"Always nice to be drunk with you." Reese nipped at my bottom lip, then deepened the kiss.

I pushed my tongue against his, tasting the whiskey between us, and I vaguely registered Shay sliding off his Daddy's lap to join River on the floor. Which set Mack in motion in a new direction. Kit didn't have to ask to join us; Mack pulled the boy down on my lap.

"I've been patient all night," Mack murmured.

The way Kit trembled turned me on beyond belief.

By the time Reese and I broke away from each other, Mack was owning Kit in a deep, passionate kiss.

I drew a ragged breath and nodded in thanks as Reese took my glass from me. Fucking hell, they were stunning together. Mack's sweet assertiveness against Kit's urgent curiosities.

"I hate to be a cockblocker," Kingsley said, "but Santa's here now."

"Santa," Kit breathed. "I wanna see Santa, Daddy."

"You will. And I'm keeping both'a y'all right here." I straightened in my seat so I could squeeze both Mack and Kit to me. Needing a taste for myself too, I gripped the back of Mack's neck and angled him my way. Then I took a hard, hungry kiss from him, tasting rum and sugar cookies on his tongue.

He exhaled a groan and tried to scoot closer.

"I'll take care of you later, boy," I promised.

He nodded and planted a trail of kisses down my jaw and neck.

Kit plastered himself to me, and he whispered in my ear, "I'm so needy, Daddy."

"I know, darlin'. Looks like you ain't the only one." Because when I glanced around the living room, it was easy to see several others were in a similar state. Hell, Noa had his head in KC's lap and was treating Daddy's cock like a pacifier. Franklin was hot and bothered by Tate and Jack making out.

Then Sloan and Luke left the kitchen right around the time Santa knocked on the door, and yeah, the two were getting along just fine. Both were visibly tipsy and happy. One aimed for Corey; the other aimed for the hallway.

I blew out a breath and did my best to get my shit together.

"All right, Littles," I said. "Try not to come in your pants."

"I make no promises," Corey snickered. "I've been looking forward to this all week!"

I bet. So had I, to be honest. Kit hadn't been sure there'd be a Santa at all. At the moment, though, his focus was split. He kept touching his own lips and sneaking glances at Macklin.

Too cute.

"Ho, ho, ho!" Greer nailed the gruff Santa tone, causing

every brat to sit up straighter. "Do we have any naughty boys in the house?"

"Yes!" Corey and Kit cried out.

"Absofuckinglutely, Santa," Tate said.

"Holy shit, I just got a new fantasy," Shay mumbled.

I grinned, glad to see Luke taking pictures.

Greer had gone all out. Not that I'd expected anything else. Perfect cushion under his big red Santa suit, no fake beard; his real beard and his eyebrows had turned white. Black boots, Santa hat a little crooked, and then...well, some kinky additions. Like the two thin bamboo canes strapped to his belt. A set of handcuffs too. A black leather flogger. Because you never knew.

"We have a chair for you here, Santa." Luke went ahead and adjusted the chair I'd positioned between the coffee table and Christmas tree. "Can I get you anything to drink?"

"Oh-ho. I won't say not to an Irish coffee." Greer patted his belly and eyed us all.

Kit couldn't sit still, he was so excited.

Archie sure was something to rest your eyes on too. Decked out in only a pair of tight black briefs and a Santa hat, he was clearly here to be his Owner's devoted elf.

"Come sit, Santa." Archie ushered Greer to the seat before the boy gathered two burlap sacks filled with gifts next to the chair.

I pressed a kiss to Mack's temple. "Can you fill me one of those snack plates?"

"Of course, Sir."

Lucian and Cam finally rejoined us after their downtime, but I kept my eyes fixed on Macklin. He worked so hard to put up a cool front, always acting casual and fun-loving. And while those traits were very much real, I knew he missed servitude. There wasn't anything he wouldn't do—so to speak—for the right Dom. For Walker.

It bothered me a great deal that they'd abandoned their marriage. They'd fucked up, both of them, plain and simple, but we'd all seen the fire between them. The kind that burned forever. Their kink dynamic had been fucking exquisite to witness. It was the vanilla aspects that'd torn them apart. Hectic lives. Macklin had been so young. Walker had lost his mother.

"Okay, everyone! It's time to start the Secret Santa reveal," Luke announced. "As you all know, Gael isn't here, so we will pass along Sloan's gift for him. Gael did drop off his gift for Sloan to Macklin before tonight, though, so no one's leaving empty-handed." He turned to Kit. "This was your project, baby. Do you have anything to say before we begin?"

"Nope." Kit just grinned. "Let the game begin! And enjoy! And merry Christmas!"

I chuckled.

"All right, then. As per Kit's earlier request—or demand— the bottoms will receive the Tops' gifts first, so that's what Santa will hand out now," Luke finished. "The floor is yours, Santa. I'll get you that Irish coffee too."

And I received my snack plate from Macklin, who just fucking knew me. Like he paid attention to everyone he cared about. Crackers and cheese, chips, cashews, and just a few sweeter treats.

"Thank you, sweetheart."

Meanwhile, Kit deserted me to go sit on Luke's lap in a chair once Greer had gotten his drink.

"Let's see what we've got here." Greer picked up the first box from the lot, and I recognized the wrapping paper. That was Luke's handiwork to Cam. "For the record, everyone's free to open their gifts right away—otherwise, we'll be here till next week." He paused and squinted at the label. "Merry Christmas, Cameron. All the hugs from Lucas. And Santa, of course."

"You remember to give Santa a kiss, darling," Lucian said.

I smirked around a mouthful of chips.

"Yes, Master." Cam blushed and climbed over a few sets of legs until he reached Santa. "Thank you, Santa. And thank you very much, Mr. West." He gave Greer a quick kiss and a hug before he hurried back to his Owner.

I already knew Cam was getting a personalized notebook that said *My Owner's Favorite Recipes* and a pair of funny socks, which was an inside joke between the two, so I kept my attention on Santa.

"Next up is Archie!" Greer declared. "Do we have an Archie here? It says Merry Christmas, sweet Archie, from Lucian."

Archie cleared his throat and grinned a little. "That's me, Sir."

Santa eyed his slave up and down. "You do look sweet. Here you go, pet."

After Archie came Franklin from KC, Gael from Sloan— saving that one for later—and Macklin from Jack. Which was great and all, but those Doms weren't in the habit of pulling pranks. KC was obviously the exception, but only on those he had that dynamic with. During their sweet, brat-less gift exchange, I finished my drink, ate my body weight in cheese and chips, and watched Noa finish his Daddy off with his mouth.

Then it was time to tune in again when Corey was summoned.

"Ho, ho, ho, it's time to set the record straight," Santa read from the label. "To Corey from Reese."

This oughta be good.

Corey was visibly suspicious on his way over. Reese merely smirked and held up his drink.

"Oh dear," Archie lamented. "I think we've reached one of your random searches, Santa."

"What!" Corey balked.

"Now, now—this is just to make sure you're not in possession of any contraband." Santa waved over his boy. "Drop yo drawers while I do a search. You can open your gift in the meantime."

I laughed. This was fun.

"Random search, my ass!" Corey yelled.

"Funny you should mention—we will actually start with your ass, son." Greer tugged the boy down over his lap and pulled down his pants, to Corey's feeble protest. "Shush. Open your gift from the nice Dom."

Stunning. I poured myself a new drink and watched as Santa forced a small butt plug up Corey's little asshole. The boy's complaints made the Sadist in me happy as a pig in shit. And it made me glance over at Luke, only to find him smirking at me. Corey wasn't the only one Greer was gonna search. This morning, we'd arranged for a surprise for Kit.

"Why do you hate lube, motherfucker?" Corey groaned.

"Corey," Sloan chastised. "That's no way to speak to Santa. Open your gift now."

The plug wasn't enough. Once it was inserted, Greer gripped his short-strand flogger and started lashing Corey's butt cheeks, to which he yelped and cried out. That sweet ass was already red from the spanking, so I reckoned it wasn't too pleasurable to be flogged there now too. But he did manage to open his gift at the same time, and we all cracked up at the avalanche of Mclean House merchandise tumbling out from a box. Mclean House coasters, pajamas, bath towels, sleeve for a laptop, stickers, and water bottles.

"Why are the jammies so soft?" Corey cried out. "I'm gonna wanna wear them, for fuck's sake!"

I laughed even harder.

"You gotta resist!" Noa demanded. "Say it with me, Corey! House. Mclean. House Mclean!"

"Be strong!" Kit cheered. "House Mclean, House Mclean!"
Oh, we best find a way to shut your mouth, little darlin'.

Kingsley about pissed himself laughing when Tate opened his
gift from River to reveal a collection of ball gags, duct tape, ear
plugs specifically for Kingsley to use, balled-up socks, a remote
with a single mute button—also for Kingsley—and gumballs so
big you couldn't speak when you chewed on one.

"I'm sensing a theme..." Tate drawled. "I don't fucking talk
too much!"

"You all talk too much," River replied into his drink.

"Aw, we have so much to play with when we get home,
baby." Kingsley hugged Tate to him and peered into the goodie
bag. "This is perfect."

Tate huffed.

And then we had Noa. He narrowed his eyes at me and
joined Santa.

"Merry Christmas to a wonderful little mutt," Santa read.
"To Noa from Colt."

"Thank you, Sadisty Sirs." Noa grabbed the box, kissed
Santa on the cheek, and returned to his seat. "Let's see how nice
Colt is."

"I'm always nice." I smiled. "Macklin agrees with me."

"Jeesh, nice spot you just put me in, Mr. Nice Guy," he
mumbled.

I ducked my head and nipped at his neck.

Santa moved on right away, this time a gift for Shay from
Kingsley.

"Oh my God." Noa started giggling at his first glance inside
the box. Soon he was pulling out a leash, a collar, a water bowl,
and a couple chew toys.

"Excellent." KC was happy. "We'll see how you enjoy fetching."

"Oh no," Noa groaned. "I'm gonna get so mad, Daddy!"

"I *know.*"

Noa tried to scowl at me, but he couldn't really hold it. "Okay, it's possible I love the gift. Thank you, Sir."

I inclined my head and leaned forward a bit. "My pleasure, son. Really. KC's already given me permission to take you out for a spin on the puppy-play course when the weather clears."

Noa was no longer happy. "Fuck."

"...and I *feel* like this is more a gift for Daddy and Master." Shay stole my focus when he unboxed...something. A notebook —okay, a journal. A nice one, at that. Leather-bound. Monogrammed too, I noticed. Except, ST for...Shay Tenley? Because I was fairly certain Shay's last name was Acton.

"It's for their enjoyment, certainly," Kingsley agreed. "But what brat doesn't love writing about his feelings?"

"Um, me!" Kit laughed.

"Yeah, seriously," Corey snickered. "That's so boring."

"The ones who don't like it are probably those who need it the most," River said. "Wonderful gift. He's gonna use it every day."

Shay sent a more genuine smile to Kingsley. "Kidding aside, I appreciate this a lot—especially the monogram. Thank you, Sir."

"What monogram?" Reese was officially lit. He squinted at the journal. "Hot fuckin' damn. Kingsley—oh, c'mere, you." He rose from his seat and stumbled over to where Kingsley and Tate sat, and that was when we started laughing. Reese was an affectionate drunk.

Before we knew it, Reese was giving Kingsley a sloppy smooch that had Tate reaching for his phone.

"Keep going," he demanded.

"Hey—ho, ho, ho-bag!" Santa hollered. "We have one more gift for a brat! Now, I don't know who Greer is, but he sure sounds handsome and incredibly intelligent. Merry Christmas, sweet little Kit. From Greer."

"That's me!" Kit exclaimed happily. "I'm sweet little Kit!"

"Kit, you say?" Archie cocked his head and tapped his chin. "Oh, right! It's time for another random search by Santa."

The look on my boy's face. He stopped mid-step and nearly dropped his jaw.

"What're you waiting for, dear? Go to Santa," Luke urged.

Kit flushed bright red and tiptoed over to Greer. "Um, hi, Santa."

"Hello, sweet boy. You can sit right here on Santa's lap." Greer patted his thigh.

I leaned back and got comfortable.

A rush of relief swept through me along with memories from our discussion about "safe" partners. Greer truly fucking was one of them. I knew exactly what was gonna happen, and I couldn't wait to witness every bit of it. Worries on this matter had ceased to exist. It was liberating as fuck.

Sometimes we just needed to screw our heads on right again.

Once Kit was positioned sideways across Greer's lap, Luke stepped closer, keeping our boy within reach.

"Have you been a good boy for your Daddies this year?" Santa began rubbing Kit's thighs a little. "You keepin' them on their toes and satisfied?"

The magic combination.

"I think so, Sir." Kit squirmed and flicked a glance my way.

I took the opportunity to undo my pants and rub Macklin's neck. I wanted Kit to know everything was fine—more than fine.

"That's good to hear," Santa said. "I happen to know your Daddies are insatiable for their little boy's pretty holes."

"Jesus," I heard Tate whisper.

Macklin leaned in and kissed my jaw. "Please let me take care of you, Sir."

I nodded and parted my knees best I could, and he sank down onto the floor between my legs.

"Do you know which holes I'm talking about?" Santa asked.

Kit swallowed hard and nodded. "Maybe my mouth?"

"That's one." Santa brushed his thumb over Kit's bottom lip, then slowly pushed it into his mouth. "Let's see how hard you can suck."

From afar, Kit's reactions seemed more forceful. His trembling, the shivers, the nerves flicking in his eyes, how he wrung his hands, and how he wriggled his toes restlessly. Sometimes it was necessary to take a step back to get the whole picture, and I had to admit I was enjoying it.

I was enjoying Macklin's attention on me too. Once my cock was out, he took over. He licked the length of it, gripped the base, and seemingly settled in to put all his focus on me.

As he eased my cock into his mouth, I combed my fingers through his hair and shifted my gaze back to Kit, Santa, and Luke—who had closed the distance. He was right behind our boy so Kit could lean back against him a little.

"That's wonderful," Luke murmured. "It's important to always be a good boy for Santa Claus."

From the corners of my eyes, I noticed several of our friends taking advantage of the situation to enjoy each other, but I had enough partners to keep track of. Greer was multitasking too. He kept his gaze fixed on Kit, who sucked greedily on Santa's thumb, but when Santa spoke, it was to Luke.

"It's nice when Daddy's a good boy for Santa too."

Oh yeah, he went there.

I smirked. Luke narrowed his eyes at Santa but said nothing, and I knew why. Luke wanted to get in on the action. He'd jumped my fucking bones right after my photo shoot with Greer, and he'd said, "Next time, use me too."

Everybody wanted a next time.

Including me.

"Daddy's willing to hear Santa out," Luke responded smoothly.

I tightened my grip on Macklin's hair, nowhere near ready to get off or even think about finishing. I slowed him down and heard Santa say something about a kiss. Whatever the exact words had been, it resulted in Luke dipping down to kiss Santa. A slow, sweet kiss that soon morphed into a sexy prelude for what we'd been discussing for "later."

Nothing was set in stone, but Luke and I had had a good talk with Greer before the party.

I exhaled as Mack swirled his warm, wet tongue around my cock, and I couldn't help but press him down on me a bit more, effectively sliding my cock deeper down his throat. Meanwhile, Santa had broken the kiss with Luke in order to kiss Kit's jaw.

"Will you lose your pajama bottoms for Santa, boy? I want to see that other hole your Daddies love so much."

"Y-yes, Sir," Kit stammered.

"I'll help you, little one," Luke offered. "Do you remember your safewords?"

Kit nodded quickly and slid off Greer's lap to shed his bottoms. Behind them, Archie gave Greer a wet towel and a bottle of oil, and then he kneeled by his Owner's side.

"Such a sweet little ass you got there, boy." Santa wiped his hands on the towel before coating a few fingers in oil. "Step closer to Santa and bend over a bit."

I cursed and sucked in a breath as Macklin became hell-bent on making me lose my shit too soon. He deep-throated me like the good cock-sucking slut he was, definitely up there in

Luke's league, and I couldn't fucking stop him. His mouth felt too good. Too warm and wet, perfect suction.

"More, Daddy..."

"Please, Master."

Heat rose within me—or maybe it was the air in the living room. Shay bent over Reese's lap to suck him off too, while River got up behind Shay to fuck him. Corey was riding his Daddy's cock and enjoying the show. Franklin looked fucking ravenous as Kingsley forced Tate's head down on Jack's cock, and Noa flew at Cam, straddling him, kissing him wildly while their Owners watched.

"Lick it, whore."

"Hurt for Daddy."

I swallowed dryly and scrubbed a hand over my face. Moans and heavy breathing mingled in the air, with Kit's sharp gasp rising above the other sounds. And I caught the moment he backed into Santa's slicked-up fingers.

"That's it—fuck yourself on Santa's fingers," Greer murmured huskily.

I met Luke's lust-filled gaze right before he got down on his knees before Kit and sucked his cock into his mouth.

Fucking hell, my mind was swimming in sex and unbidden images of what might happen in the future. Corey riding Sloan's cock was hot as fuck, even more so when I locked eyes with Sloan and let myself wonder if there'd be a day I could have both him and Luke writhing under me. Sloan was goddamn gorgeous, and I bet he loved to take Greer's cock as much as Luke loved to take mine.

Kit whimpering stole my focus, because I knew that sound so well. He was close. He was being such a good boy, fucking himself desperately on Santa's fingers while Luke swallowed his cock.

Just seeing them pushed me closer to the edge, and it was as if Macklin sensed that. He redoubled his efforts, causing me to tense up. *Fuck, fuck, fuck.* It messed with my head to see sex everywhere; it threatened my composure and lured out the animal in me. The same animal who loved to hunt down my boy in the woods and rapefuck him till he screamed and came all over himself.

When I felt Reese's hand on my thigh, I acted on instinct. He looked about as caged as I felt. We met somewhere in the middle and kissed hungrily, as if one more sexual act would set us free. Just one more, just one more. His warm, demanding tongue against my own, our heavy breaths filling the nonexistent space between us, our frustrations rolling off our shoulders.

I groaned as Macklin rolled my balls in his hand, squeezing them just right to set me off.

"Keep goin', pet," I growled. "Swallow every drop."

Reese cursed and planted his forehead on my shoulder. "Now, Shay. Swallow Daddy."

I was already gone. The euphoria exploded around me and pulled me under, and I fucked Macklin's throat, pushing deeper with each release of come that burst from my cock.

Christ almighty, I'd need some R&R after this.

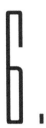

6.

"Oh, *Colt*." Luke gave me the look I'd been expecting as I came down the stairs tightening the drawstrings of my sweats. "We're in the middle of a party, for goodness' sake."

"I lasted till nearly ten. You should be proud." I smacked his cheek and gave him a quick kiss on my way to the kitchen.

Fucking excuse me, but I had limits. After Macklin had sucked the energy out of me and the whole living room was smelling of sex, the party went in a new direction for me. One, I was done playing dress-up. Two, I was switching alcohol for coffee and soda. Three, I was equal parts full and starving.

Besides, I wasn't the only one changing clothes. The majority of the brats and subbies were in either pajamas or sweats. Reese was walking around in boxer briefs and handing out Band-Aids, and Franklin was stark naked.

While Kingsley and River finished their smoke break, I heated up some leftovers in the kitchen and grabbed a Coke.

"Daddy!" Kit came running in, breathless. "Can I eat and sit with you, please? I miss you."

Aw, my baby. "You never have to ask, little darlin'. Come here."

I picked him up and positioned him on the only available

surface next to the coffeemaker. His cheeks were still flushed from all the excitement, but I detected some uncertainty in his eyes too.

"Talk to Daddy. Everythin' okay?" I checked the microwave, but the food needed another minute or so.

I'd wanted to have a quick aftercare chat with Kit earlier, but he'd been busy giggling and fawning over his new pajamas that Greer had given him. Custom-designed fighter jet PJs, like a whole suit in the softest material—I believed it was called a onesie. Only, it came with a detachable hood in the same fabric, same design, that covered his face except his mouth. "Because sometimes, only those two sweet holes matter," Santa had said. So a hole to insert Daddy's dick in the boy's mouth, and a flap in the back for the other Daddy to pump his cock in and out of the boy's ass.

Wonderful gift.

"So much yes, but I wanted to make sure you're okay also." Kit tugged at my hand. "I don't want you to worry that I...you know... I don't know. Maybe that I'd want more of...outside play with Tops? And I don't."

He was too sweet. I planted my hands on the counter, caging him in a bit, and I kissed his nose. "That's the thing, Kit. I'm not worried anymore. And if you do want to explore some dirty fun with someone else in the future, we'll get through that together."

I was more convinced than ever before, and that was because I'd finally listened to Kit. He wasn't naturally open with his relationships. He wasn't Macklin. He wasn't overly adventurous. He was...more like me. And even I could appreciate some extra spice from time to time.

I was curious about his wording, though. "You enjoyed your scene with Santa, didn't you?"

There was that sweet blush.

"Considering how fast I came..." He laughed a little at himself. "It was so hot, Daddy. But it kind of stays there...? I don't know if that makes any sense. I just feel like...this was so darn sexy, and I'm glad I got to experience it. But you and Daddy are the only Doms I want to be intimate with beyond...I guess what Greer did out there. I wouldn't want to go any further with him—or any other Top."

Despite that I wasn't worried anymore, that felt fucking incredible to hear. Especially since I was the same. I related to his line of thinking.

"You're very sweet for checkin' in on Daddy," I murmured. "I'm glad you told me this. It makes me very happy. Do you know how much Daddy loves you?"

He smiled, every trace of uncertainty gone, and widened his arms. "This much?"

I shook my head. "Way, way more."

He giggled. "How far do I have to hold out my arms?"

I pretended to think about it as I checked the food again. Now it was perfect—and there was plenty for Kit to eat too.

"From here to Pluto," I decided.

Kit gasped. "That's funny, because that's how much I love you too."

Christ, what did he do to me? When he said things like that, I lost control of my own reactions. With a single goofy smile, he could squeeze my heart till it almost hurt. And I craved the sensation.

"It's settled. We love each other from here to Pluto." I kissed him on the forehead and helped him off the counter. "Let's go steal our corner on the couch before Corey comes back from cleanin' out his asshole."

"Oh my gosh, Daddy!"

"What? That's what boys gotta do after Daddy's done with

them." I didn't exactly think Sloan had used a rubber with his own boy. "Come on."

"Yeah, but—" Kit huffed. "You use very vulgar words sometimes."

Because it made him blush.

For the second half of the Secret Santa game, I got greedy. I planted myself in my spot of the couch, Kit on my left, Macklin on my right, and Luke on the other side of Macklin.

If possible, the food was even better now. River, Kingsley, Jack, Sloan, and some of the boys agreed with me as they joined us with their own plates. And by then, Greer was officially jealous and itching to get out of the Santa suit. He'd already shed the pillow stuffing and unbuttoned the top.

"May I get you a plate too, Santa?" Archie asked.

Greer weighed his options. "I'll eat later when we're done here. Maybe a cookie and a water for now."

"Right away, Sir." Archie scurried off.

"Here comes the fighter jet." I made an impressive jet sound and flew a forkful of food to Kit's mouth. That never failed to amuse him.

"It's so quiet and peaceful now," Reese noted. "Did Noa pass out?"

"Shut up, meaniepants," Noa bitched. "I'll punch you."

He wasn't passed out—*yet*. He was close, though. Snuggled up between KC and Lucian with a blanket and a stuffie. Cute as fuck.

"There will be no punching on my watch," Santa said. "Okay, new bag, new set of gifts. It's time to find out what the brats have been up to this month."

"I thought Santa knew everything." Shay smirked.

Santa frowned. "Shut up, meaniepants. I'll punch you."

"Remind me again of the difference between brats and Sadists," Luke muttered. "Because I don't see one."

I waved my fork at him. "Sadists make the rules."

"Only if they're also Doms," he pointed out smartly.

Dick.

"All in favor of Lucas shuttin' his trap?" Santa asked.

"Aye!" We'd cast our votes. Moving on.

Santa was suddenly impatient, so he went for three gifts at once. From Gael to Sloan, from Shay to Kingsley, and from Archie to Lucian. And I zoned out a bit, more interested in my food and Kit snuggling up against me. He was getting tired too. It'd been a long day.

"May I put on my clothes again, Sir?" I heard Franklin ask quietly. He looked good on the floor, I couldn't lie.

"Why?" Jack combed his fingers through Franklin's hair. "Are you cold?"

"No, I just—"

"Then no." Jack smiled.

"Jesus Christ," Kingsley blurted out.

"I'll second that," Lucian said.

I furrowed my brow and shifted my attention to those who'd just opened their gifts.

"What's the matter?" KC wondered.

Kingsley gusted out a breath and raised his brows, then revealed...an old book. And a fancy-looking pen.

"My, my, that looks like a first edition, Master," Tate said.

"Archie gave me a set of engraved cuff links and a very nice tie." Lucian cleared his throat and shifted in his seat. "This is incredibly generous, pet."

I narrowed my eyes at Kit, who was refusing to make eye contact.

Sloan was equally moved by Gael's gift, a pair of custom-designed All Stars and what looked like a 3D-printed figurine. Four, actually. Four little characters standing together.

Those bratty fucking shits. This was their plan. To one-up us, to be *thoughtful*...after we'd given them kinky, tongue-in-cheek gifts.

Oh, but the joke was on them. Sort of. We had a plan B. Clearly, we'd need to execute it.

Jack, River, and Luke were up next, and Archie handed out their presents. Macklin had gifted Jack a cooking class at his restaurant for two—Franklin as well. From Tate, River unwrapped a mailbox. An actual mailbox. Oh, it was for their house. It was painted on too.

"My students helped me paint it, Sir," Tate murmured. "That's you and Reese holding hands with Shay—and Shay's last name peels off, you know, for obvious reasons."

"Aw, that's sweet." Luke smiled.

It really fucking was.

River opened the mailbox and exhaled a laugh. A handful of ramen cups fell out.

This wasn't solely Tate's idea, was it? He'd picked out Shay's gift for Kingsley. The brats had all teamed up.

"You don't know how much this means to me." River cleared his throat, visibly uncomfortable. "Thank you."

Tate beamed in satisfaction.

Reese draped an arm around his brother and kissed the side of his head.

"I'm gonna remember the looks on your faces forever," Noa snickered sleepily.

I set aside my plate. I had to prepare myself. If Kit had helped Noa pick out something for me, chances were it was going to hit all the feels.

I side-eyed Luke, who was smiling at his own gift. It was

buried in silk paper, so I had to lean over Macklin to see what it was.

Turned out, it was several things. A Christmas ornament that read, "Our first Christmas together." A picture frame with a photo of Luke, Kit, and me from this summer. We'd been sitting on our porch outside our cabin in Mclean. Mid-conversation, mid-laughter, with Kit on Luke's lap. Last but not least, a stack of vintage frames for "a lifetime of family moments."

It was my turn to clear my throat, 'cause that shit just got to me. And I glanced over at Reese, Greer, Kingsley, all the Tops—just to make sure we were on the same page. A few subtle nods did it. We were definitely adding plan B to the roster.

"I can't really find the words," Luke admitted. "Thank you so very much, sweetheart."

Cam grinned. "You're welcome, Sir." The secretive glance he exchanged with Kit right after confirmed my suspicion.

"All right. Uh..." Santa stepped on it and hauled out the last boxes. "To KC from Franklin, to Reese from Corey, to Colt from Noa, and to Greer from Kit."

Fuck me if I wasn't a bit nervous all of a sudden.

It didn't escape my notice that Noa was watching me, all while sucking on his thumb on KC's lap.

It also didn't escape my notice that the box Archie was carrying toward me had "Handle with care, this side up!" written in all caps on every side of the blue snowman-printed wrapping paper.

Okay, let's see what Noa and Kit had been up to.

I placed the box on my lap and tore off the paper, then carefully lifted the lid.

Kit leaned in and bit his thumbnail.

As soon as I saw what it was, I shook my head and didn't fucking know how to react. Sweet mother of amazing boys. My heart thumped a little faster, and I had to swallow hard as I picked up the glass case with an indescribably important model aircraft set on a stand inside. Indescribably important to me. This was history. This was...Kit.

I remembered the first time I'd brought him down to Norfolk to meet my folks. He'd gotten stuck on a photo in their hallway, a picture of my old man and me, standing in front of this very jet. The T-38 Talon. The first jet I'd ever flown in, back when my pop was an instructor. Then the first jet I'd had my own pilot training in.

This right here was the last drop, the very thing that'd made me proclaim that I was going to be a pilot like my father one day.

I turned the case in my hands, and I grinned at the memories flooding me. All the nerves, the sleepless nights of studying, the first hours you got to log, the debriefs when you were so goddamn tired you almost fell asleep right where you stood.

This was why I couldn't retire just yet. Not fully. I wasn't ready for a morning when I woke up, knowing I'd never fly again.

I glanced at Kit, finding him smiling softly at me.

He did know what this meant to me. He knew exactly.

"I love you so damn much, boy."

His smile widened. "I love you too, Daddy."

"There's more in the box, Sir," Noa said. "Something that's actually from me."

I wasn't ready to let go of the case. Hell, the hours Kit must've put in on this model—in secrecy, to boot. The work was just out of this world. Down to the smallest details and markings. Reluctantly, I let Kit hold the case so I could see what Noa had left me at the bottom of the box.

A smaller box. A much smaller box. I opened it and cocked my head, sure I'd seen this before. It was a tiny, pocket-sized book, and it reminded me of the album my ma kept of all the newspaper clippings... Shit, it *was* that album, only downsized to fit in the palm of my hand. I flipped through the pages and saw copies of every entry my mother had put in the original album. News article from the day I'd earned my wings, another article from the time I'd almost crashed in Iraq—a news story that'd made Luke worried sick. We'd only shared a single night together at that point, right before I'd deployed.

"Kit and I drove down to your parents' a few weeks ago," Noa revealed. "Your mom makes the best lemonade in the whole world, by the way."

I smiled widely.

Kit took over. "She showed Noa the album, and he was like, yeah, let's replicate this so he can have one at home too."

"She could probably talk about you and your sister for weeks without a break." Noa laughed softly. "I totally friended her on Facebook, just so you know. She and I are pals now."

I couldn't believe them. "I'm blown away," I admitted. "Thank you, both of you."

And yeah, my ma made the best lemonade in the world.

"Then perhaps you can stop calling me your oldest friend?" Franklin suggested.

I laughed.

Noa scratched his nose. "I don't know, Mrs. Carter looks pretty young. How can I be sure you're not older?"

"For heaven's sake, I'm the same age as Colt, practically," Franklin argued.

Noa rolled his eyes dramatically. "*Praaactically.* Whatever you say, boomer perv."

Ah, Noa, the comic relief we loved and adored.

As I looked around the living room, it was easy to tell that the boys' thoughtful gifts had taken the fight out of us. I bet it'd be a while before we terrorized the little ones again. At least a day or two.

I couldn't see Reese's and KC's gifts, but I understood why Greer was hugging the ever-loving shit out of his boys. Next to his chair leaned a wrought-iron sign that said Finlay Ridge Family Farm. And...I could only assume Kit was responsible for the Osprey model kit—or as he liked to call it, a Jarhead Taxi. And Greer was certainly our favorite jarhead.

"That was a nice stunt you pulled, brats," I said. "I give it an A+ in emotional torture."

"Amen," Reese agreed.

"At the least." Greer nodded. Greer, not Santa. He'd taken off the hat and dragged a towel over his beard and eyebrows. "It's a good thing we always have an ace up our sleeves."

"No!" Noa yelled. "No aces, no more tricks, we won! We fooled you!"

"But we don't play by your rules, little one," Luke pointed out. "Your gifts were so incredibly meaningful that we must make you suffer."

I loved that man so hard.

"Un-fucking-fair!" Corey cried out.

"Jesus Christ, they're fucking with us," Shay grated out. "Calm yourselves."

Ha! Ah, Corey's scowl now was something else.

"I'm calm," he snapped.

"That's enough, boys," Sloan said. "It's a good surprise, I promise."

I nodded for Reese to take the wheel.

"All right, you bratty li'l fucks," he said. "Y'all better know how to swim because we're all going on a cruise in March. Down in the Bahamas, we'll see what blinds you the most, the sun or River's lily-white ass."

I winced at the sudden victory shout of a hundred brats expressing their excitement. Holy shit, I should've put in earplugs.

Mack sighed. "So *this* is why you should have a Dom."

"Oh my God, I wanna swim with sharks!" Noa exclaimed.

"Oh my God, I don't!" Corey mimicked.

I shook my head in amusement and refocused on Macklin. "You're a fool if you think we haven't included you, pet. We've already bought the tickets."

We just hadn't known beforehand if we'd be announcing the trip tonight or some other night the brats decided to bamboozle us.

He perked right up. "Really?"

Oh, come on. We weren't leaving our Mack behind.

"I'm *so* ready for this trip," Tate said. "I can barely remember the last time I saw sunlight."

Safe to say, the rest of the evening would be spent discussing a cruise. And whether or not we were swimming with sharks.

Franklin and Jack were the first to leave around midnight, and Tate and Kingsley followed shortly after. KC and Lucian's brood went back and forth on whether they were staying the night or heading back to their condo across the river, but in the end, they opted to go home.

The Finlay Foursome decided to split up for the night. Sloan and Archie were beat and wouldn't mind some downtime before they picked up the kids tomorrow, so at almost two AM, they wished us a merry Christmas and headed for Corey's place in Arlington, leaving Greer and Corey behind to spend the night here.

Around that time, River, Reese, and Shay said goodnight and went upstairs to sleep. And Corey and Kit begged for a movie night.

"Movie night *now*?" Luke asked. "It's two in the morning,

boys."

"Pleeeaase, Daddy?" Kit begged and clasped his hands together. "After tonight, I won't see Corey until next year!"

Oh Christ.

Macklin snorted a chuckle and carried some bowls and trays out to the kitchen.

"You can decide after we've showered, Kit," I said. "If you're not half asleep by then, you can watch a movie."

"Okay! I *won't* be too tired."

We'd see.

I nodded toward the stairs. "Let's go, then. Corey, you know where your guest room is?"

"Yes, Sir. I'll go help Dominus in the shower also," he replied. "Now that Reese is gone, I might dare try my new propaganda jammies."

I chuckled. As if we wouldn't take a picture and send it to Reese.

Kit and I made it up to our floor and aimed straight for the bathroom. When he asked me *not* to pee before the shower, I knew what he wanted, so I merely nodded and removed my clothes.

It'd become a once-in-a-while comfort for him, and lately, for me too. I'd never been interested in watersports before him, and I still wasn't—except for this one routine he and I shared. Sometimes when he'd had a long day, sometimes when he was feeling emotionally wrung out...

Kit yawned and stretched his arms over his head. "Are we gonna play more tonight, Daddy?"

I hummed as I tested the temperature of the water. "Play might be a strong word. Luke and I talked to Greer when you were sayin' goodbye to Tate and Kingsley, and we came up with a plan for next time, so to speak. But it doesn't have to be tonight. We were kinda talkin' in terms of after the holidays."

I stepped in under the hot spray and let out a long breath as the water soaked me in seconds. Jesus, that felt amazing.

Kit joined me and asked about said plan.

"That we establish a set of boundaries in which we can test the waters," I replied. "With you and Corey, for example. Like we decided before, you're free to do whatever you want with him so long as y'all stay safe. And Macklin—he's a safe play partner for all of us. But we stay within those lines. Greer's family and Macklin, nobody else for now. Otherwise, it's easy—like tonight—you find yourself in a situation where many of your friends are havin' sex, and in the heat of the moment, you want to push a limit you might regret later. Lust has a way of changin' one's mind."

Kit pondered that and got down on his knees before me, and then he nodded firmly. "That makes sense. Macklin did tell me it was always best to go slow."

Macklin was right, of course.

"But I don't know that we need this written in stone or anything," he added. "I'm not interested in anybody else."

That may be, but it was always best to have an official agreement, which I explained to him.

"Okay, fiiine. No more talking now, Daddy." Boy got a little huffy. "I mean, except for comfort stuff. That's my favorite."

I snorted and grabbed his no-tears shampoo. Fair enough. "Only comfort stuff," I confirmed. "I don't think Daddy can get hard yet, though. I'm still beat after Macklin."

"Mmm, I wish I could've seen more than his head going up and down..." He plastered himself to me and sucked softly on the head of my cock. "You and Daddy have the best cocks in the whole world."

I grinned faintly and started massaging the shampoo into his hair.

"I like the idea of Macklin being my kink brother," he

admitted in between kisses to my cock. "Cuz then I can say that my brother sucked on Daddy's cock before I did."

Christ. That sure sent desire through me, in a thick, sluggish wave.

"Maybe you and your brother can suck on it together sometime," I murmured.

"I would love that." He shivered and closed his eyes, humming at the pleasure of having my fingers in his hair. I rubbed his scalp too, the way he loved it. "I'm so happy, Daddy."

My turn to shiver. Hearing him say that meant everything to me. "That's our goal in life, little darlin'. For Luke and me to always make sure you're happy."

"Mmm, my goal for my Daddies too..." He flicked his tongue against the slit of my cock before he tilted his head up in silent permission. Silent request.

He wanted to be covered in Daddy.

I took a deep breath and lowered the water pressure just a bit. Then I gripped my cock and let go, directing the stream across his shoulder. His neck. Chest. And his other shoulder. Across every tattoo that covered the skin on his upper body.

He smiled serenely, keeping his eyes closed.

"That's a good boy." I touched his cheek lovingly, the water slowly washing away the shampoo suds. "Daddy and I meant to tell you—you've been amazin' all day. Not a single hissy fit."

He grinned goofily. "I *never* do that."

I exhaled a chuckle and groaned a little too, 'cause it felt so damn good to relax. "Daddy's all done now, baby. Let's clean off."

He snickered behind his hand, then squinted up at me. "Remember the time you called me your little piss baby?"

I laughed and hauled him off the floor. "I remember how squirmy and horny you got. You were like, oh my gosh, Daddy, can you breed me right fuckin' now?"

He laughed too and shook his head quickly. "I didn't use those words!"

Eh, close enough.

The humor faded as we cuddled up under the hot water and washed each other. Like all the other times we'd showered together recently, he said he wanted my chest hair to grow back quicker, because chest hair produced more suds with the body wash. And I told him, not for the first time, to let that be a lesson. Don't fuckin' tell Daddy to shave again, not even for a photo shoot.

"Yeah, I know," he sighed heavily. "I can't always be a genius."

Hoo boy, he was taking after the fighter pilot there a bit. No wonder Luke called him Mini Colt sometimes.

"I think I need to start callin' you li'l junior," I chuckled.

Judging by how Kit's eyes lit up, he was a fan.

About ten minutes later, we'd toweled off and put on our comfy clothes again, and Kit jumped up on my back before we headed down the stairs.

He wasn't tired enough, so the movie night was happening.

Kit peppered my neck with smooches. "We're going to Florida soon," he sang. "But first, Christmas!"

"That's right. We still have to find some more stocking stuffers for Luke."

"How about tomorrow after my lunch with Vincent?" he suggested.

"Did you text him already?"

"Yes, we're going to the Italian place next to the ice cream shop I really love. What's it called again?"

Considering he loved all the ice cream places in DC, I had no damn clue.

And it didn't matter; it was a good plan. But also, Jesus Christ, Luke and Macklin had been busy. The living room was spotless. Two black trash bags stood in the entryway doorway, both presumably filled with gift wrapping.

"Hellooo, anybody here?" Kit slid down and landed on his feet, and I peered into the kitchen.

Empty—wait. There was a note attached to a tall stack of dirty plates.

We're in the backyard.

-L

Huh. "Kit, grab your coat and boots. Mittens and beanie too."

We went out into the entryway and bundled up good and proper, and then we grabbed our boots and walked back through the living room and dining room. And the first thing I saw through the patio door was the grill. It had to be Greer who'd started a fire. Sure as heck wasn't my city boy.

We'd only been gone fifteen, twenty minutes, and in that time, it was like leaving one party to attend another one altogether.

"What's Daddy up to?" Kit asked curiously.

"I don't know. Let's find out." I got down on one knee and helped the boy tie his boots. Otherwise, he'd just ignore it and end up tripping. Which I didn't need with a covered pool nearby. With Kit's luck, he'd fall right in.

I stood up again with a grunt and opened the door, and my eyebrows went all the way up there. Hell, they'd cranked up the coziness out here, that was for sure. They'd brushed the snow off the two big sunbeds, extended the sunroof, and lit torches along the patio.

"You showered *forever*," Corey accused.

Luke smiled back at us. "There you are. We have coffee and cocoa."

"Aw, yesss!" Kit ran over.

"And soda!" Corey added.

There was a lot more than coffee and cocoa, I'd say. *And soda.* They must've emptied the house of blankets, and I was pretty sure I spied a bag of chips in Greer's lap. So that's what I dove for. This summer, right after we'd entered Kit's life, it'd been him and Luke on that sunbed. Now it was Kit, Corey, Macklin, and Greer swapping body heat to stay warm. And they better make room for Luke and me.

"Comin' through." I gave Luke's ass a squeeze on the way because it called to me. "What sparked this idea?"

Corey grinned sleepily and crawled up on Greer's lap. "I love watching the snow fall. We've started having cocoa on the porch at home whenever it snows."

"That's a fine tradition." I could imagine copying it, 'cause this was nice. I dropped a kiss on Macklin's forehead and climbed over him, then hauled Kit onto my lap so Luke could squeeze in too.

We should buy heaters.

We were fairly protected from the harsh winds, partly because of the house itself, the wall, and the tall bushes and trees that framed the narrow backyard. But definitely still cold out here.

Luke ended up on the other side of me, and he told Macklin to cuddle up between his legs, which I thought the boy needed. Macklin needed to be tended to, cared for. And Luke was the perfect man to go into Daddy mode for Mack too.

"What a way to wrap up the party." Contentment swept through me, and I let out a big breath. "I'm glad y'all decided to spend the night."

Mack extended two Yeti cups to Kit and me, and I took a sip

of the perfect coffee and leaned back against the cushions.

"Oh, there's marshmallows in," Kit whispered. "I love, love, love marshmallows."

We knew. Boy could go through a whole bag in one sitting.

A comfortable silence fell over us, and for a while, we just enjoyed the moment and watched the snow fall across the yard. The pool was buried along with the lawn.

The street on the other side of the wall was silent.

Luke drew a few blankets higher up and kissed the top of Mack's head.

"I could probably fall asleep right here," Mack mumbled.

"Me too." Kit slurped audibly from his cocoa and finished with a satisfied, "Ahhh."

"Yeah, so who wants a snowball fight?" Corey asked.

"I do!" Kit raised a hand.

"Forget it," I chuckled. They couldn't lure me down under a bunch of blankets and then think I'd be remotely interested in throwing snowballs.

Neither were Luke and Greer—or Macklin, for that matter. But the Littles were undeterred, so they willingly left our fortress of warmth to dart out onto the blanket of snow.

"You make sure to stay away from the pool, boys," Luke warned.

"Yes, Sir!"

"Let's make snow angels first, Kit. Okay?"

"Yeah, okay."

I sighed contentedly and drank my coffee, and Greer scooted closer.

"Share the heat, Texan."

"Heat is a stretch," I drawled.

"Feels plenty hot to me," Mack teased.

I grinned and took me another swig of coffee. A beat later, Macklin hitched a leg over Luke's and mine, and I rubbed his thigh absently under the blankets. In the meantime, Kit and Corey were making snow angels on the lawn.

"It's fuckin' bonkers how much I love that boy," Greer murmured. "I'm embarrassed sometimes to think I didn't believe it would be possible at first."

I knew what he was talking about. He'd fallen so hard for Archie and Sloan, and Corey had entered their lives in a new way when they'd already had so much going on. But the boy fit right in with them.

"We're happy for you, buddy." I leaned over and gave his cheek a smooch. "You only had to wait ten years, and then you got three of them in the span of a few weeks."

He chuckled warmly and tilted his face toward me. I smirked a little, then brushed my lips to his. The boys wouldn't even begin their snowball fight if Greer and I took this any further.

"Finally," Luke sighed.

I didn't know what he was referring to. Scooting down in my seat, Greer and I deepened our kiss at the same time, and I extended my coffee to whoever was willing to grab it. Probably Mack.

Then it suddenly hit me—Luke was waiting for me. He was the one with all the patience, so he let me take the lead. And what he'd been waiting for was playtime.

I broke away and glanced over at Luke and Mack. "Get over here. Lord knows Greer and I won't take care of each other's needs."

Greer barked out a laugh and welcomed Luke in his arms a few seconds later. "Yeah, this is better. Someone I can actually stick my cock in."

"Oh, please don't talk. You ruin everything then." Luke smirked and covered Greer's mouth with his own before there could be any wisecracks in response.

"Are we done discussing limits?" Mack crawled on top of me instead, and I nodded and captured his mouth in a hard kiss.

"You and Greer are safe for Luke and me," I said. "You and Corey are safe for Kit and Luke."

Mack grinned wolfishly. "I feel so special."

"I dig those limits." Greer was quick to roll Luke onto his back instead. "But, Colt...? You'll probably hear from Sloan soon."

Fuck, yeah. "Lookin' forward to it." I had nothing else to say. I went back to kissing Mack, and I slipped a hand down his sweatpants—that he must've borrowed from Luke. "Hard already? Shocker." I wrapped my fingers around his smooth cock and stroked him quickly.

He gasped and groaned into the kiss. "You've been teasing me all goddamn night. Sir."

"Quiet." I shuddered at the cold and realized pretty fast that this wasn't gonna work.

As nice as the snow-watching idea had been, I needed us indoors and on a more pliable surface. The thick, soft rug in the living room was probably perfect. We'd have the couch right there too.

"Fuck this, we're headin' indoors," I said. "Mack, you help me move the coffee table, and then I want you naked."

"Yes, Sir. Right away."

Luke and Greer were thankfully on the same page.

"Boys! Join us when you're ready," Greer hollered.

Two Littles popped up like meerkats from the snow.

"Holy smokes," was the last thing I heard from Kit.

Then I ushered Macklin inside and unbuttoned his jacket as I pushed the tip of my tongue into his mouth. He moaned and pressed himself closer to me, his fingers working fast to remove my clothes too. Shoes off, coats off, I hauled his tee over his head, then tore mine off in the next go.

"At long last, Colt's decided to share this fine ass with me," I heard Greer mutter.

I threw a glance over my shoulder. "Don't go easy on that ass-slut."

Luke was beyond ready. His expression screamed *fuck me.* "I hope we can find enough condoms."

Oh right. Yeah. I cleared my throat and scanned the living room, as if I was gonna find a single rubber there. Christ.

"Corey and I are always prepared. I'll send him upstairs," Greer said.

"Tell Kit too," Luke added, out of breath. "I think we have a few in the bathroom."

I tuned them out and focused on lifting the coffee table out of the way.

"I have a single rubber in my wallet, and it goes on your big fat cock as soon as we land on the floor," Macklin informed me.

I nodded, and we lowered the table next to the tree. "All right. Then I beat the shit outta you for tryin'a boss me around. Deal?" I didn't give him any room to respond. Instead, I closed the distance between us and grabbed him by the throat, only to whisper in his ear. "The only thing you're gettin' if you keep that up is my big fat belt. You hear me, boy?"

"Fuck," he whimpered. "I'm sorry, Sir. I just got excited."

"You can get excited again once you know your place." I kissed his cheek and let him go. "Get the rest of your clothes off and kneel on the rug."

"Yes, Sir." He lowered his gaze and returned to the couch.

Upon seeing Greer pushing Luke down onto the floor, I took a deep breath and tried to will time to slow down. If we were engaging in group play, I needed it done right. It couldn't be over in five minutes.

"We gots to hurry, hurry, hurry," Corey panted, running up

the stairs with Kit. "How many condoms do you have? I always have a pack in my bag. I think there are twelve or something."

"Don't wake up the Tenleys," I warned.

Another couple deep breaths. Time to take control of the situation.

After dimming the lights some more, I stepped out of my sweats and joined Mack on the rug. Then I sat down on the floor, in the corner, and reached out to smack Greer's ass.

"Get down here so Mack can tell you where his place is," I told them.

Greer hummed and dragged out the deep kiss he shared with Luke. "Doesn't he know his place is wherever we tell him it is?"

"You'd think." I glanced over at Macklin.

"It's been a while since I was submissive," the boy said in his defense.

I grinned and draped my arms along the edge of the seat cushions.

Greer rumbled a laugh and got off the couch to join me on the floor. Luke wasn't far behind, and he crawled between my legs to give me a kiss.

"I love you," he whispered.

I smiled against his lips. "Love you too, darlin'. Be a good slut for Greer."

"I'll take both of you." He kissed his way down my chest, and I drew in a breath and placed a hand on the back of his head. His mouth on my cock followed, and I lolled my head back, enjoying the warm-up.

Greer tended to Luke's warm-up instead. Kissing his spine, playing with his ass, taking off his pants. Clothes were off-limits on the rug, I decided right then and there.

The boys were good. They hurried back down to us with condoms, oil, damp towels, and lube, and I told them to strip.

"Toss me a rubber, baby," Greer said.

"Yes, Owner." Corey was happy to oblige. "Where do you want me?"

"Just jump in the pile, son," I said. "I know for a fact that Luke can't get enough cock."

"There you have it." Greer rolled a condom down his cock and positioned himself behind Luke. "Something you wanna say to us, Macklin?"

I groaned as Luke sucked me harder, and I felt his loud moan sending vibrations up my length when Greer pushed inside him. Fucking hell, that was incredible. So was Kit, when he reached my side, completely naked, not showing any signs of discomfort about his skin being on display. He'd come so damn far since this summer.

"I apologize for acting demanding, Sirs," Macklin said. The remorse in his voice helped.

"Hi, Daddy," Kit whispered, excitement brimming in his eyes. He lifted one of my arms to sit down on the edge of the couch, and he kissed my hand and smiled down at me.

Gorgeous.

"Lift your leg so Daddy can get a taste," I murmured.

No matter what we did tonight, I wanted everybody close to me. I wanted skin on skin, heavy breathing, and sweaty bodies writhing. Kit obeyed like the good boy he was, and then I leaned toward him and sucked his hard, cute cock into my mouth.

"Oh!" He trembled. "Maybe you want to come over here to me, Corey?"

"Heck yeah." Corey didn't waste a second, and soon he was seated next to my boy. "Do you also wake up sometimes in the middle of the night because someone is sucking or fucking you?"

"It definitely happens." Kit struggled to sit still. He was so physically sensitive sometimes, and he could get off in a minute.

I swirled my tongue around his cock, coating him properly,

and sucked him hard.

In the background, I heard Greer give Macklin permission to stroke Luke, but I kept my gaze on the boys. They were beyond adorable, neither of them knowing quite what to do next. Corey brushed a finger over Kit's arm and told him he loved the tattoos. In turn, Kit blushed and tentatively placed a hand on Corey's thigh.

Corey wasn't as shy as Kit could be, though. He took the next step and kissed Kit's neck. "Okay, I'll be honest. I think you're so damn hot."

I smiled and kissed the inside of Kit's thigh before I let them have their first moment together.

Kit had his own confession to make, about the crush he had on Corey, and that sealed the deal. They met in a tentative kiss, just a few brushes of their lips, until Corey deepened the kiss a little with a swipe of the tip of his tongue.

Their sweet innocence was a stark contrast to how Luke deep-throated me as if there was no tomorrow.

"Sit back on Greer's cock," I told him quietly.

It was the last order I gave. From then on, I just wanted to take.

We'd be here till the sun rose, wouldn't we?

I couldn't care less.

Lying flat on the floor, I had Luke draped over my left side and Macklin on the right. Kit was bent over my cock, sucking me for all he was worth, while Corey fucked him hard and instinctively.

"You can multitask, boy." Greer inched closer and guided his cock into Corey's mouth. "That's it, breathe through your nose."

I stretched out with a long groan and combed my fingers through Kit's hair, feeling him bobbing up and down to please me. I fucking loved having all these hands on me. Blunt nails raking down my chest, teeth grazing my nipples, tongues teasing my balls. Luke captured my mouth in a lazy, toe-curling kiss, only to push me toward Macklin next. He tasted of chocolate and mint and was eager to get everything he could. And in mere seconds, he'd take a railing from Luke.

I was done lying still. I sat up and kidnapped Kit's asshole from Corey, who looked endearingly pissy.

"Watch it, son." I snapped my teeth at the boy and coated my cock in lube. Then I forced Kit down on the rug and pressed my cock between his cheeks.

He cried out through a moan.

"Always so perfect," I whispered against his neck. "Let's get you closer to your new brother so you can show me how much you like him."

"Yes, Daddy," he pleaded.

Luke had heard me, so we met halfway, in the center of the rug, where Kit and Mack could reach each other while we fucked them.

I peered down between us, where my glistening cock disappeared in and out of Kit's clenched asshole, and I couldn't describe the sheer hunger that took control of me. I couldn't get enough, and I couldn't stick to one position. I wanted everything at once. I wanted to be consumed by everything we did, and I wanted my mind to swim. Or drown, whichever.

———

That center-of-the-rug pile was where it was at. That was where I found the unbridled, animalistic euphoria and got completely fucking lost in the moment. Where time didn't exist. Where Kit lost his voice riding my cock, shyness long gone, all while Corey stood in front of him with his cock in Kit's mouth. Greer railing Macklin right next to me, Lucas stroking and rubbing my skin as Macklin deep-throated him.

I groaned and gripped Kit's hips tighter, needing him to go faster.

The younger generation had already gotten off—fucking twice—and it was my turn. Luke had come all over Macklin's beautiful face too. Which Kit and Corey had licked off. I was strung tight and ready to blow, and by the looks of it, so was Greer.

Macklin was moaning like a whore, the sounds muffled by Luke's cock.

"I'm close again, Daddy—I can't help it," Kit whined.

Say no more.

I sat up and lifted him off me, and I didn't really care how he landed. Because then I hauled him up on all fours and forced my way in again, and I fucked him for all I was worth. He let out a wail of pain and pleasure, but the pleasure won out when Corey literally stuck his head under Kit's body so Kit could fuck Corey's mouth at the same time.

"Oh my God, oh my God," Kit panted. "Corey, I'm gonna come. Oh my God."

"*Fuck,*" Greer growled. His ass was a fucking work of art as he pumped into Macklin's ass.

Luke stared hungrily at Corey's body on display. With a gorgeous boy on his back, naked, there wasn't a chance in hell Luke could resist. He withdrew from Macklin's mouth, rolled on a condom, and stepped between Corey's legs.

The sight was too much. Corey's shock, how his abs tensed when Luke gathered the boy's legs around him and pushed his cock inside became my undoing. Maybe Kit's too. As sweat trickled down my neck and chest, I screwed my eyes shut and let the forceful sensations claim me. I buried myself all the way in, and the orgasm crashed down on me.

Macklin's desperate moans fueled me, as did Corey's breathless whimpers, Greer's gritty curses, and Kit's hoarse cry.

Holy fuck, my knees, my thighs, every goddamn muscle hurt. Thank God—Luke had the brains to pull Corey out from under Kit, because I collapsed on top of our boy as soon as my climax faded.

"We should probably go to bed..." That was Luke.

In a minute.

I yawned and kissed Kit's neck, my cock still buried inside him. But we had company now. Macklin was performing cleanup service and had his face pressed between us, his tongue licking the base of my cock and around Kit's opening.

I scratched Macklin's scalp absently, a big fan of the teasing licks.

Corey had fallen asleep on top of Greer, who was running his fingers lazily up and down the boy's back and sweet butt.

"I'm not sure I can carry him up the stairs," he murmured drowsily.

"Fuck that," I chuckled. "We're on the third floor. I can carry Kit down the stairs, not up."

"You have before," Kit yawned. "Ohhh, that tickles, Macklin." He wriggled his butt, and that was enough for my cock to slip out.

It was also an invitation for Macklin to swallow me. A fan of ATM, evidently.

"I can walk myself." Corey's words were so drenched in sleep, I could barely decipher them. "What time is it?"

I grunted and rolled onto my back, allowing me to check the

clock in the window. Jesus Christ. "Four thirty."

"Definitely time to go to bed," Luke said firmly. Then promptly groaned when he sat up. "I hurt *everywhere*."

Kit snickered. "I thought you were young, Daddy."

"Oof," Greer laughed. "Right in the kisser."

Luke sniffed. "I'm just going to pretend I didn't hear that."

Macklin released my cock and kissed his way up my chest. "Tonight was...on another level."

I smiled and kissed him softly. "It sure was."

Beautiful boy.

"I'm gonna order an Uber," he said quietly.

That made me frown. "What? You're stayin' with us."

He shook his head. "I actually feel good, so you don't have to worry or anything. But I want to be with my boy."

Oh. Well, I couldn't very well stop him. "I thought he had a date."

"He's home again." He kissed me once more before he sat up and scanned the surroundings, maybe for his clothes. "I'll see you in a few days in sunny Florida, though."

"Oh my gosh, I can't wait." Kit stretched out alongside me and cuddled up in my arms.

"We'll let you go on one condition," Luke told Mack. "You'll call us in the morning. We want to be able to check in with you."

"Of course, Sir. I know the drill." Mack turned a little cheeky, and he rose from the floor and kissed the side of Luke's head in passing. "Now I'm just gonna hunt down my clothes... Colt, where did you throw my jacket?"

"Because I remember that," I drawled.

Everyone chuckled tiredly.

"Never mind, found it."

All right, then. Our bed was waiting for us. On the third floor. Two hundred steps away. Fuck me.

EPILOGUE

"**I**t's time to go!" I hollered for the hundredth fucking time.

We were supposed to be off to the airport... I checked my watch. Fifteen minutes ago.

I was ready. I'd put all the luggage in the entryway, I'd ordered a car to drive us, and I'd packed the Christmas presents for my sister and her family. We were visiting them right after our vacation to Ty's house south of Naples.

Luke joined me in the hallway. "Please be patient, sweetheart. You know how he's been the past few days."

Yeah, I knew, but I didn't want us to miss our flight.

Kit had regressed a fair bit after the holiday party. We'd actually seen it coming, though maybe not to this degree. We'd just barely managed to get through Christmas dinner with my folks, then Christmas brunch with Luke's parents.

Right now, Kit had zero interest in being an adult. He was clingy—and that part, I fucking loved. I had no complaints. The uncertainty, however...? Fuck. And we'd been prepared for that too. Again, maybe not to this degree.

It wasn't uncommon for people to go the opposite direction after a major event, such as taking part in group play. We'd talked and talked, and we'd made sure he didn't have any regrets, which he didn't. In fact, he'd gained a dose of boldness and now flirted with Corey via text.

At the same time, he was extremely anxious and didn't want to be away from us for more than a few minutes. He was essentially going through the Little version of what I'd gone through with both him and Luke. How I tightened my hold before I could relax. In short, Kit needed some reminding that we were solid as a triad.

"Daddies! I can't find my fighter jet jammies!"

Luke returned to the living room and called up the stairs. "I already packed them, love!"

"Oh. Okay! Then I'm ready to go!"

Praise Jesus.

If I could just get him and Luke on the plane, I could smother the boy in cuddles and whatever other reassurances he needed. And then some. I had no problems whatsoever repeating comfort a million times. It was part of my identity as a Daddy Dom. *If I could just get them on the damn plane first.*

"I'll head up," Luke said. "We really need to go."

Really?

While I waited, not-so-patiently, I fired off a text to Macklin. He'd eventually decided to bring his boyfriend, so that should get interesting. None of us had met him before. He wasn't from our community.

We weren't on the same flight, though, so introductions would wait till we got down there.

The doorbell rang before I could send the text, and it was just perfect. Now the driver was chomping at the bit. He was gonna start charging extra before Kit had even put on his shoes. I opened the door...and did a double take.

Well, fuck.

"Walker," I blurted out.

He smirked faintly. "It's been a while, friend."

Well, *fuck*.

Colt, Kit, and Lucas continue to cross over throughout the Game Series.

But now it's time to hear from Macklin, Lane, Ty, and Walker.

MORE FROM CARA

Next up in the Game Series

Apex Predator

Lane/Ty & Macklin/Walker

Primal Play | Capture/Takedown | Consensual Non-Con | Possessiveness | D/s | Group Play | Tentacle Play

Cara freely admits she's addicted to revisiting the men and women who yammer in her head, and several of her characters cross over in other titles. If you enjoyed this book, you might like the following.

Out

MM | Comedy Romance | Coming Out Story | Age Difference | Standalone

I had two things on my list when I arrived in Los Angeles. One, track down Henry Bennington, the uncle and guardian of my little brother's best friend Tyler, and tell him to get his ass back to Washington—because his nephew was getting out of control. And two, figure out just how non-straight I was. Nowhere on this list did it say, "Get Tyler's uncle into bed and fall for him." Nowhere.

Out for the Holidays
MM | Sequel to Out | Comedy Romance | Family | Adventure

I'm not saying Henry jinxed us when he sent out approximately two hundred holiday cards stating that we were going to have a blissful Christmas at home. But somewhere between going to Mexico to deal with work and the man who didn't want me and Henry together, and then heading to Philadelphia because someone thought it was a good idea to run away, I decided that I'm writing the damn card next year.

Power Play
MM | Daddykink Romance | Age Difference | Mental Health | Standalone

Love sucked. Correction: it sucked when you were in love with your parents' closest friend and he didn't feel the same. Madigan had always been there for me, from when I was a kid to when I got drafted by the NHL. Then I made the mistake of confessing my feelings for him... I was such a loser. My bipolar disorder was already difficult to manage as it was; add high anxiety and, most recently, as the cherry on a shit sundae, a suspension from the team. Why couldn't he see that I was perfect for him? We even had kink in common! Not that he knew that...

The Guy in the Window
MM | Mild Kink | Age Difference | Taboo | Standalone

I was in the middle of my divorce when Adam messaged me. I believe his exact words were, "Hi. I think you're my dad's brother. Would you like to get to know me?" My brother and I had never been close, so I'd only met his adopted son a few times when he was very young. First, he became sort-of-my-nephew. Then he became the guy who helped me find an apartment, coincidentally across the alley from his own place. Then one night, as I got ready for bed, he became the guy in the window.

Check out Cara's entire collection at www.caradeewrites.com, and don't forget to sign up for her newsletter so you don't miss any new releases, updates on book signings, free outtakes, giveaways, and much more.

ABOUT CARA

I'm often awkwardly silent or, if the topic interests me, a chronic rambler. In other words, I can discuss writing forever and ever. Fiction, in particular. The love story—while a huge draw and constantly present—is secondary for me, because there's so much more to writing romance fiction than just making two (or more) people fall in love and have hot sex.

There's a world to build, characters to develop, interests to create, and a topic or two to research thoroughly.

Every book is a challenge for me, an opportunity to learn something new, and a puzzle to piece together. I want my characters to come to life, and the only way I know to do that is to give them substance—passions, history, goals, quirks, and strong opinions—and to let them evolve.

I want my men and women to be relatable. That means allowing room for everyday problems and, for lack of a better word, flaws. My characters will never be perfect.

Wait...this was supposed to be about me, not my writing.

I'm a writey person who loves to write. Always wanderlusting, twitterpating, kinking, cooking, baking, and geeking. There's time for hockey and family, too. But mostly, I just love to write.

~Cara.

Get social with Cara
www.caradeewrites.com
www.camassiacove.com
Facebook: @caradeewrites
Twitter: @caradeewrites
Instagram: @caradeewrites

Made in the USA
Monee, IL
14 January 2023

25045399R00089